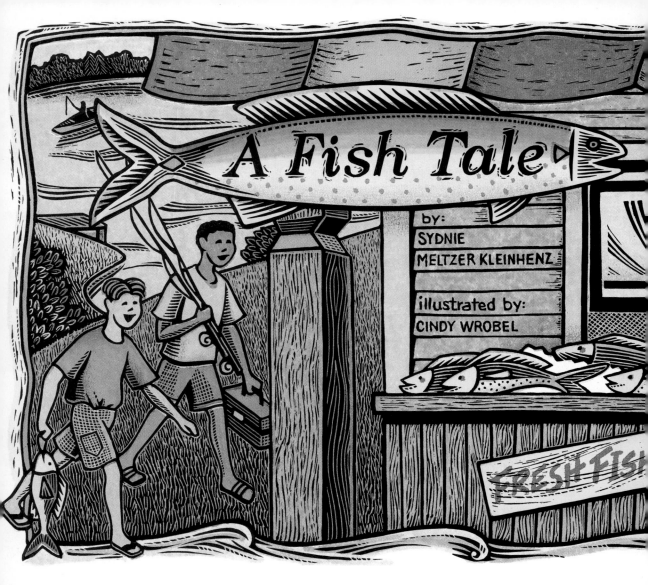

A Fish Tale

by:
SYDNIE
MELTZER KLEINHENZ

illustrated by:
CINDY WROBEL

FRESH FISH

Ingrid was down by the lakefront one day when she saw Sam and Travis emerge from the brush. Sam swung a tackle box and held their two fishing poles. Travis grasped a line with a fish on it.

Ingrid hovered close by. "Will you let me fish with you?" she asked.

Sam didn't like Ingrid. Her name and the way she spoke were foreign to him. Did she come to Kansas just to bug him?

"No, no, and no, in case you still ask," Sam said with authority.

"I know all things to do," Ingrid said. "When we fished in Finland, my dad said I had a gift for catching big ones."

"Our fishing spot is just for us," Travis said. "We made a vow. No one else must use it."

"Go hug a slug," said Sam.

Five times Ingrid asked to fish with them. Five times she got a no. Then she figured out a plan.

The next day, Ingrid ran with her fishing pole to Al's Fish Shop. She got a big catfish, slipped off to a hiding spot, and strung it on her line. She was stationed on the path when Sam and Travis came back from the lake.

"Incredible!" said Travis. Sam stared with suspicion.

"That's some fish!" said a man.

8

The man snapped a shot of Ingrid and her fish.

"I'd like to investigate where you got that," Sam said.

"From the lake," said Ingrid. "I will take out the bones at home."

Travis said, "You know how to cut up fish by yourself?"

Ingrid nodded. "Oh, yes!"

"That's a good skill," Travis said. "We could go fishing sometime."

Sam poked him. "What about our vow, Travis?"

Travis shrugged.

Travis and Ingrid went fishing and pulled in some bass. Sam got mad seeing Travis with Ingrid. He tossed rocks into the lake to make a commotion and scare off the fish.

Ingrid and Travis put down their poles. As they got up, Ingrid slipped on some mud. Travis grabbed for her and tripped on a rock. Into the lake they plopped! When they emerged giggling, Sam jumped in with them. They all swam and had fun until they were exhausted. Then they squished off home, dripping wet.

The next day, Ingrid was in the *Lakefront News*! "That's you and your catfish!" Sam said to Ingrid. "I'll get you one of these for a souvenir."

Ingrid blushed and bit her lip. "Oh, Sam and Travis! I did a bad thing. I tricked you. I got that fish at Al's shop." She looked ashamed.

Travis said, "We're glad you told us! You're our pal now, Ingrid from Finland." Sam nodded.

"Oh, thank you!" Ingrid said. "Now come with me to *Lakefront News*. I want them to tell my big fish tale!"

Think About It

1. Why do you think Ingrid wanted to fish with Sam and Travis and not by herself?

2. Why don't Sam and Travis get mad when Ingrid says that the catfish came from Al's shop?

3. The *Lakefront News* prints a story about Ingrid and her big catfish. What do you think it says? Write a story the *Lakefront News* could print.

Prefixes and Suffixes

Understanding prefixes and suffixes can help you read new words. A **prefix** is a word part added to the beginning of a base word. A **suffix** is a word part added to the end. These word parts can change the meaning or part of speech of a word.

Prefixes:	un-	re-	mis-
Suffixes:	-ful	-ly	-less

Read these sentences. What suffix can you find in the first sentence? What prefix can you find in the second sentence?

> Ingrid felt **hopeless** about getting Sam and
> Travis to take her fishing.
> She **misled** them about the big catfish.

Now read these sentences. Which word has a prefix? Which word has a suffix? What do these words mean?

> Ingrid didn't want to be unfair to Sam and Travis.
> She told them the shameful story about her fish.

Add a prefix or a suffix to each word in the box. Write a sentence with each new word you make.

kind	do	place
cheer	quick	help

13

THE QUIVER

by Sharon Fear
illustrated by Leslie Wu

Will was lost.

How had he let this happen?

Someone's wagon wheel had broken, so all the wagons had stopped. Without telling Ma or Pa, Will had jumped down and run into the trees, just to look.

That's when he had seen the quiver. Did it belong to a Blackfoot hunter? What an incredible souvenir it would be of this trip!

Will had investigated the creek next, looking for things there. And when he looked up. . . he was lost.

How often had Ma said sternly,
"Don't run off without telling us.
You'll get lost"?

How often had Pa, looking solemn,
said, "If you get lost, you must not panic.
Stay in one spot. We'll find you"?

But Will did panic, running and
falling. The trees and rocks all looked
the same! He found himself weeping—
he just couldn't help it.

A blurry image emerged from the trees. What was it? Will interrupted his sobbing. When the image was less blurry, he could see that it was not an "it," but a "he."

Someone just his size was kicking up leaves and moss. It was clear that he was looking for something.

He looked sad and solemn and about to weep himself. Then he sat down and did just that.

Will realized that he was looking for the quiver. It looked ordinary to Will, but maybe it wasn't ordinary to that boy.

Will composed himself and got up. Hearing Will's tread, the boy jumped up, too, and stepped back. Then, seeing the quiver Will held out, he reached for it.

The boy brushed his hands across his wet cheeks. Then he stepped close and looked at the wet tracks on Will's cheeks. Will had seen his feelings. Now he seemed to see Will's.

The boy looked puzzled when Will got a stick and made lines in the mud. Then he realized what Will was saying with them. *Have you seen a wagon and a team of oxen?*

The boy grinned at Will, gave him a signal to come, and ran off. Will ran to catch up, and they jogged on without speaking. A mile or so on, they broke from the trees and climbed up on some rocks.

Will could see well from here. No hills or trees interrupted the flat land, but the deep ruts of wagon wheels did. To the west, Will could see the wagons.

He gave a yell and ran down into the long grass. Then he looked back and waved.

The boy who had helped him lifted the quiver one time. Then he melted back into the trees.

Will's parents did not criticize him for getting lost. They just hugged him and let him tell his incredible tale.

"The quiver seemed to mean a lot to that boy," said Pa.

"Maybe his ma made it for him," Will said. "Maybe his pa gave it to him. I just know he was very glad to get it back."

"Not as glad as we are to get you back," said Ma.

She didn't exaggerate—Will could tell.

Think About It

1. How does Will help the boy he meets? How does that boy help Will?

2. Do you think Will feels bad that the boy has seen him weeping? Why or why not?

3. That night, Will writes in his diary. He writes about what happened and how he felt. Write Will's diary entry.

The Audition

by Susan McCloskey
illustrated by Linda Pierce

Jean looked at the clock on the wall. It was close to ten, when the audition would begin. The hall was filled with kids who hoped to get into the music show. Chad was clutching his trumpet, Jan had set up her drums, and . . . oh, no! There was Aldo with his cello!

This was going to be a problem. Jean also played the cello, and the music show needed just one.

Jean had rehearsed and rehearsed for the audition. She realized that Aldo must also have rehearsed a lot. Jean did not flatter herself that she played well. Still, she hoped she'd win the audition.

Miss Small, who led the music class, walked in. All the kids stopped talking.

"I'll call you up to audition one at a time," Miss Small said. "The rest of you, please be patient and sit still."

"Aldo, you can go first," Miss Small called out.

Aldo sat up in his seat. He nodded to the accompanist, a pianist, and they began to play simultaneously. The notes of a sonata filled the hall.

All of a sudden, Aldo stopped playing, grimaced, and jumped up. The accompaniment came to a halt as well. One of the strings on Aldo's cello had broken!

25

"Do you have a spare string, Aldo?" asked Miss Small.

"No, ma'am," Aldo said.

Jean smiled to herself. Aldo had just begun his sonata when the string broke. It was as if he hadn't come to the audition at all! Now all she had to do was keep from making blunders in her waltz.

Then Jean stopped to think. If she won the audition, would it be best for the music show?

"Bad luck, Aldo," Miss Small said. "Jean, you're next."

Jean got to her feet. "Miss Small," she said, "if it's all right with you, Aldo can use my cello to finish."

Miss Small smiled. "Thank you, Jean," she said.

Jean smiled, too. Maybe Aldo would win the audition, but she felt that she had done what was best for the music show.

1. Why does Aldo suddenly stop playing the sonata?

2. Why does Jean feel that she has won when Aldo stops playing? Why does she feel that she has done what is right at the end of the story?

3. What do you think happens at the end of the audition? Write down your ideas.

Vocabulary in Context

When you read, you may come to a word you don't understand. In many cases, other words or pictures in the story can help you understand the new word. Those helpful words and pictures are **context clues**.

Reread these sentences from "The Audition."

> He nodded to the accompanist, a pianist, and they began to play simultaneously. The notes of a *sonata* filled the hall.

How do the highlighted words help you know what *sonata* means? These context clues help you guess that a *sonata* is a musical piece.

Now reread this sentence from "The Audition," and look at the picture. What does the word *grimaced* mean? How can you tell?

> All of a sudden, Aldo stopped playing, *grimaced,* and jumped up.

Choose four words from below. Find out what each word means. Then write a group of sentences using each word. In your sentences, give clues to the meaning of the word.

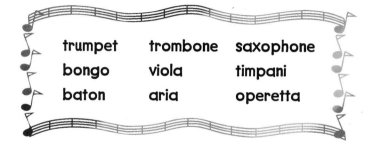

trumpet	trombone	saxophone
bongo	viola	timpani
baton	aria	operetta

Lessons *from* Barbara Jordan

by **Kana Riley**

illustrated by **Stacey Schuett**

FROM: Jane Barr
TO: Wilma Downs
DATE: 10/12/00 07:58 PM
SUBJECT: Grandma's Technology!!!

REPLY   SEND   TRASH

Grandma,

    I'm so glad you have started to use e-mail. I like sending and getting mail fast! Do you?

    Grandma, can you help me? I have to tell my class about Barbara Jordan. Mom said you met her one time. What was she like?

Love, Jane

FROM: Wilma Downs
TO: Jane Barr
DATE: 10/13/00 06:15 PM
SUBJECT: Barbara Jordan

REPLY   SEND   TRASH

Jane,

    I did meet Barbara Jordan. She was making a speech. That speech inspired me! I was glad to meet a smart woman with such dignity and confidence.

    Did your mom tell you about Ms. Jordan's career?
Love, Grandma
P.S. How far we have come! Correspondence was not this fast when I was ten. This e-mail technology is lots of fun!

FROM: Jane Barr
TO: Wilma Downs
DATE: 10/13/00 08:15 PM
SUBJECT: Barbara Jordan's Career

REPLY   SEND   TRASH

Grandma,
     Mom said that Ms. Jordan sat in Congress.
What else did she do?
Love, Jane

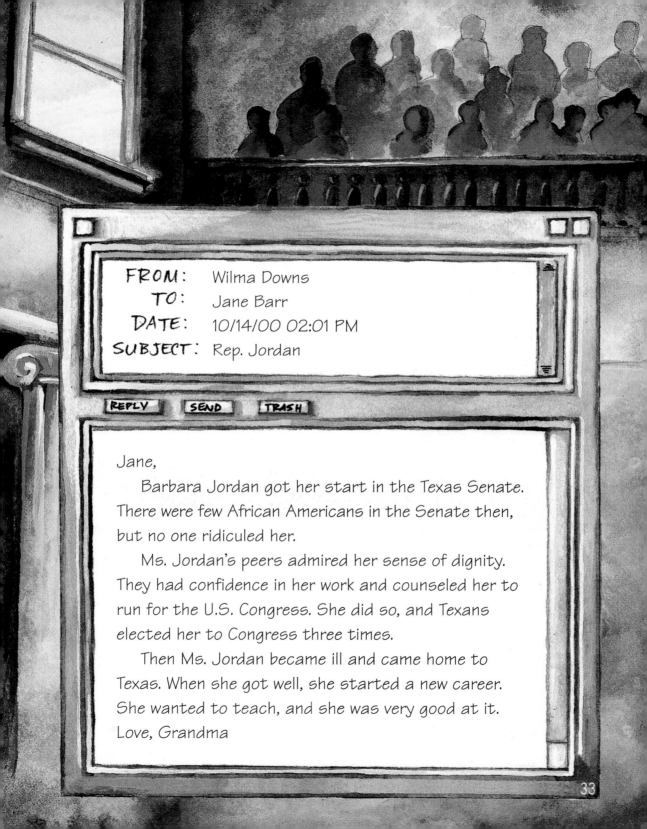

FROM: Wilma Downs
TO: Jane Barr
DATE: 10/14/00 02:01 PM
SUBJECT: Rep. Jordan

REPLY   SEND   TRASH

Jane,

Barbara Jordan got her start in the Texas Senate. There were few African Americans in the Senate then, but no one ridiculed her.

Ms. Jordan's peers admired her sense of dignity. They had confidence in her work and counseled her to run for the U.S. Congress. She did so, and Texans elected her to Congress three times.

Then Ms. Jordan became ill and came home to Texas. When she got well, she started a new career. She wanted to teach, and she was very good at it. Love, Grandma

FROM: Jane Barr
TO: Wilma Downs
DATE: 10/14/00 04:50 PM
SUBJECT: Barbara Jordan

REPLY   SEND   TRASH

Grandma,
    Thanks for all your help. I looked up Barbara
Jordan on the Web, too. Now I have lots of facts
about her life.
Love, Jane
P.S. I hope the class likes my talk!

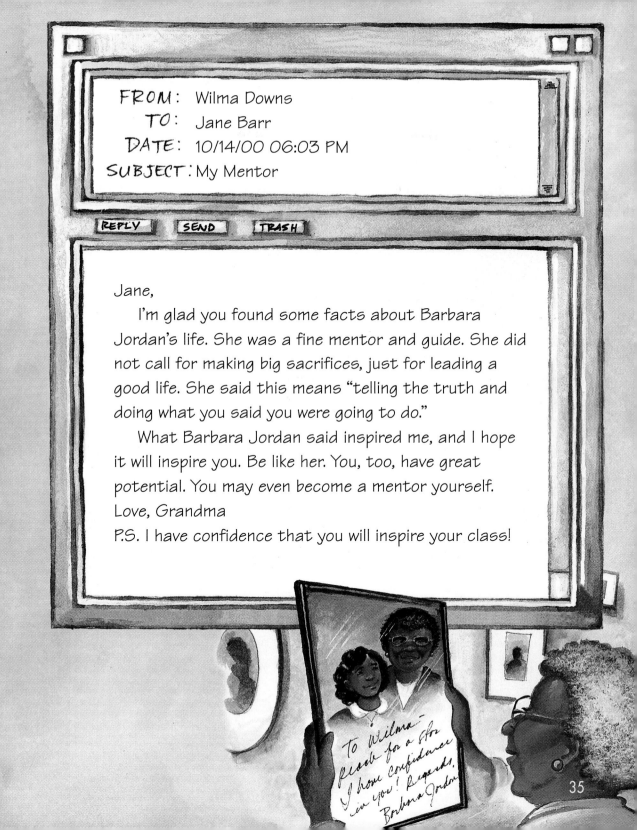

FROM: Wilma Downs
TO: Jane Barr
DATE: 10/14/00 06:03 PM
SUBJECT: My Mentor

REPLY   SEND   TRASH

Jane,

I'm glad you found some facts about Barbara Jordan's life. She was a fine mentor and guide. She did not call for making big sacrifices, just for leading a good life. She said this means "telling the truth and doing what you said you were going to do."

What Barbara Jordan said inspired me, and I hope it will inspire you. Be like her. You, too, have great potential. You may even become a mentor yourself.
Love, Grandma
P.S. I have confidence that you will inspire your class!

FROM: Jane Barr
TO: Wilma Downs
DATE: 10/16/00 07:52 PM
SUBJECT: TA-DA!!!

REPLY   SEND   TRASH

Grandma,

I got an A+ for my report on Barbara Jordan!
The class liked my talk a lot. Now they want to
hear what else she did for humanity. Will you come
to class and tell us all about her?
Love, Jane

To Wilma -
Reach for a star.
I have confidence
in you! Regards,
Barbara Jordan

A+

Think About It

1. Why does Jane ask her grandma about Barbara Jordan? Why does she also look up Barbara Jordan on the Web?

2. Why do you think Barbara Jordan made a good teacher?

3. Jane's grandma comes to class and talks about Barbara Jordan. After that visit, Jane sends another e-mail to thank her grandma. Write the e-mail Jane sends.

That Day Last Week

by Lisa Eisenberg

illustrations by Jill Arena

One day last week my pal, Mike, and I were planning to ride our bikes. In my memories, that day started out okay. I put on my helmet and rode over to Mike's. When he came out, he looked at the helmet in disbelief. "Are you going to keep that thing on all day?" he asked.

I grinned. "Yup. I think it looks neat. Besides, if I happen to fall, I do NOT want to scramble my brain!"

"Well, I'm leaving mine at home," Mike said. "It makes my head hot, and I hate the way I look in it. Come on, let's go!"

"Okay, okay!" I said.

Now, I wish I had used better judgment. I should have said "No way! I'm not riding bikes with you unless you put on your helmet. Maybe I'll just go by myself."

Instead, I just said "Okay," and we were on our way.

39

We rode in the park and down by the lake. We did all our routine things, and it seemed like a very good day. Then Mike sped away from me down Lake Street. I couldn't see him, but I could hear him yell "Oh, no!" Right after that, I heard a crash.

By the time I got to Mike, he was flat on his back. A man and a woman were jumping out of their car. "I didn't see him!" the man said. "He rode right out in front of me!"

"He didn't hit the car very hard," the woman said, "but he landed with a hard impact." She seemed very upset.

My reaction was one of disbelief. It had all happened so fast! Was Mike okay?

Mike was taken to the hospital, and I went home and waited for news. Each time there was a call, I jumped up in anticipation. "I just wish I'd made Mike put his helmet on," I said to my mom.

"You need to keep things in perspective, Andy," she said. "You're not Mike's dad. You couldn't make him put his helmet on. You had *yours* on. It was Mike's judgment that was bad, not yours."

At last Mike called. "I'm home now and making a fast recovery, Andy. I just needed some stitches. My mom and dad are mad that I didn't have my helmet on. I came close to getting killed!"

"I wish I'd made you put it on," I said to him.

"Well, I'm going to from now on. I'm with you—I do NOT want my brain scrambled!"

"Next week we're going to start a bike club in our class," Mike went on. "Mr. Gray visited me. He'll be the sponsor. He says I can go up to the podium and tell the kids what happened to me. Then I'll talk about safe bike routines—like using helmets!"

"Neat!" I said. "When can I come over and help speed up your recovery?"

"Come over now! And if you're riding your bike, please—put on your helmet!"

44

Think About It

1. How would the story be different if Andy insisted that Mike put on his helmet?

2. Why do you think Andy doesn't insist that Mike put on his bike helmet? What would you do?

3. What do you think Mike will say when he goes to the podium and speaks about safe bike routines? Write the speech he will give.

The Pirate Hero

by David Lopez
illustrated by Liz Sayles

When Roberto Clemente first came to the Pittsburgh Pirates in 1955, he made a vow—he promised himself that he would play hard for the team.

In 1971, the Pirates were playing a set of games with the Baltimore Orioles. One of these teams would be the best team in baseball.

Some people said the Pirates couldn't beat the ace lineup of the Orioles. To Clemente, that was an error. His team was going to win!

The Pirates went to Baltimore for the first two games. The billboard at the ballpark read "Home of the Orioles." Filled with confidence, the home team won game 1. Pirates fans looked solemn when their team lost game 2 as well.

For the next game, the team was glad to be back in Pittsburgh. There the billboard greeted the Pirates, and fans hoped the team could make a comeback.

An Oriole error helped the Pirates win game 3. That was fine, but it wasn't time for them to boast yet—they had to keep winning!

Led by the man with the 21 on his uniform, the Pirates won games 4 and 5.

Now the games went back to Baltimore, and people there said the home team would win again.

In five games, Clemente had gotten at least one hit a game. In game 6, he got two hits—one of them a home run. But the Orioles still won the game.

Clemente got one hit in game 7. It was a home run, and this time the Pirates won the game.

The games were over, and the Pirates were the best team in baseball for 1971! Clemente was a hero to Pittsburgh fans.

Clemente was a star to *all* baseball fans, and they praised his fine playing. He was glad to have the praise, but he didn't boast. He had just kept his promise to play hard.

Roberto Clemente was a hero in and out of baseball. When he wasn't helping his team, he was helping people in need.

For example, Clemente met someone who needed to get artificial legs. Clemente gave some of the money himself. Then he helped raise the rest of it.

In 1972, Roberto Clemente lost his life. It happened when he was helping people. Clemente was taking help to some people who needed it. The plane crashed after take-off—the control tower did not see it going down.

The people of Pittsburgh dedicated a statue to Clemente. The artist sculpted him in his uniform with the number 21 on it. Fans can visit the statue and dream that Roberto Clemente is still playing for the Pirates.

Think About It

1. How did Roberto Clemente help the Pittsburgh Pirates? How did he help other people?

2. Why do you think Clemente didn't boast? How do you think that made the fans feel about him?

3. Think about Roberto Clemente. Make a web with words that tell what he did. Then write a paragraph describing Roberto Clemente.

Draw Conclusions/Make Generalizations

In some stories, the writer does not tell you what a character does or how a character feels. You have to look for facts that can help you figure out these things. You can use those facts, plus your own experience, to **draw conclusions** about the characters.

This chart shows how you could draw a conclusion about Roberto Clemente in "The Pirate Hero."

Story Facts		**My Experience**		**Conclusion**
Clemente promised himself that he would play hard for the team.	**+**	People who make promises to themselves really want to do well.	**=**	Playing well for his team was very important to Roberto Clemente.

When you read, you can also look for patterns in the way characters act or the things characters say. When you find patterns, you can **make generalizations**.

This chart shows a generalization you might make when you read "The Pirate Hero."

Pattern		**Generalization**
Even when his team is down, Clemente keeps doing his best.	→	Clemente is a person who does not give up.

Write a paragraph about a baseball player or another athlete. Tell what that athlete does, and give clues to how he or she feels.

ROOKIE ROBIN

by Tomas Castillo • illustrations by Allen Garns

Jeff Gates had hopes of making the Robins. He was one of five rookies in training with the Robins this season. Last year he had played with the Hawks.

For Jeff, this last training game was the big test. Lots of fans came out to the gigantic stadium. The game was a bargain for them—it was free!

In the first inning, Jeff fielded a line drive. He could hear some clapping along with the murmur of the fans.

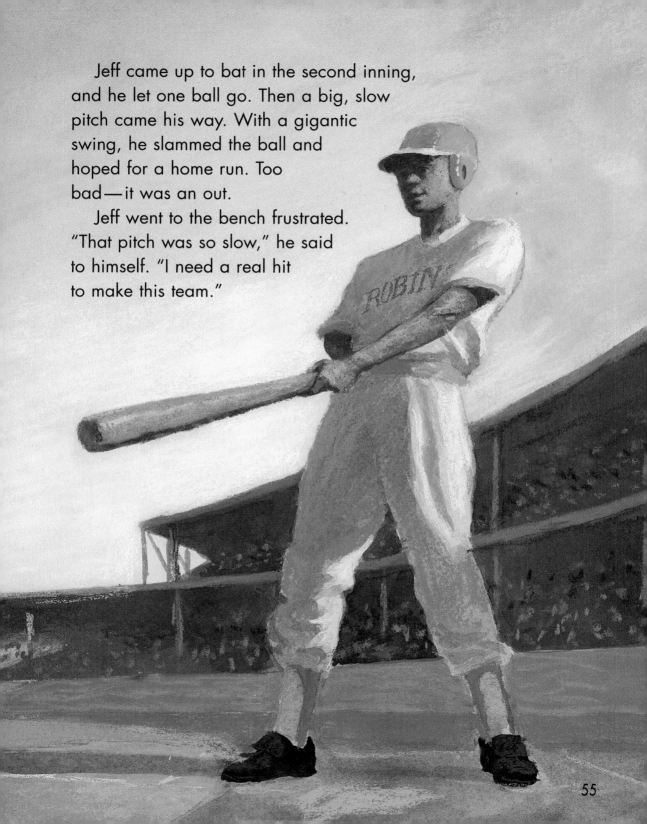

Jeff came up to bat in the second inning, and he let one ball go. Then a big, slow pitch came his way. With a gigantic swing, he slammed the ball and hoped for a home run. Too bad—it was an out.

Jeff went to the bench frustrated. "That pitch was so slow," he said to himself. "I need a real hit to make this team."

In the fifth inning, a pitch came so close to Jeff that the ball deflected off his leg. He was not pleased to get on base that way. That pitch was no bargain. He needed a big hit!

Jeff made an out in the seventh inning, but no one cheered. "No one roots for me," he said to himself. He felt bad.

In the last inning, Jeff went to the equipment box and picked out a new bat. He did not blame the equipment he had used, but maybe a new bat would help him get his big hit.

The Robins needed that big hit, too. They had made an out on a pop-up. They had made a second out on a strikeout. Then they got two hits and a walk.

When Jeff came to bat, he was introduced as a Robin. Jeff liked that. The Robins fans clapped—they were rooting for him! He wanted so much to make the team. He didn't want to blow it!

The first pitch sped in, and Jeff swung hard and hit it. The baseball looked like a home run down the line. Then a gust of wind got it, and it landed on the far side of the pole.

Jeff came back to the plate. He let three balls go—they were wide. "Let me have a pitch to hit," Jeff called out.

"Time out!" the umpire called. The coach was on his way to talk to Jeff.

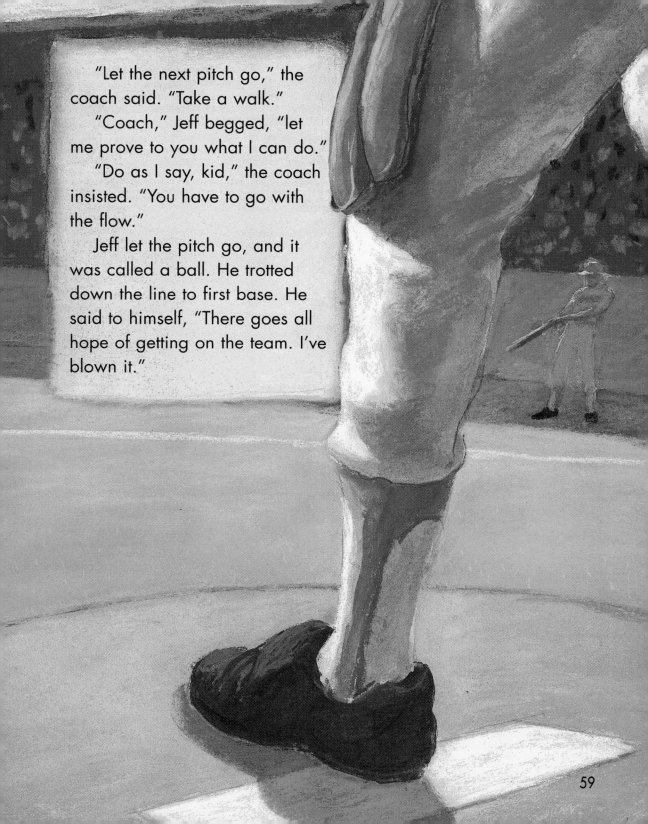

"Let the next pitch go," the coach said. "Take a walk."

"Coach," Jeff begged, "let me prove to you what I can do."

"Do as I say, kid," the coach insisted. "You have to go with the flow."

Jeff let the pitch go, and it was called a ball. He trotted down the line to first base. He said to himself, "There goes all hope of getting on the team. I've blown it."

When the game was over, Jeff was told to go and see the coach. As he waited, he spotted a big trophy in the hall.

Then the coach came out and saw Jeff staring at the trophy. "We got that for team play," he said. "Your team play today got you on the Robins."

"My team play?" Jeff was puzzled.

"When you let that pitch go, you were playing for the team," the coach said. "That's what we need."

Jeff grinned. He realized he hadn't blown it after all. He was so happy to be on the Robins!

Think About It

1. Why does the coach think Jeff would make a good Robin?

2. In the last inning, how does Jeff feel about doing what the coach asks? After the game, what does Jeff find out about what he has done?

3. Jeff writes to his grandpa, telling him what happened at the game. Write Jeff's letter.

RACE FOR LIFE ON THE
IDITAROD TRAIL

by Caren B. Stelson

It is 1925 in Nome, Alaska. The wind is blowing, and the snow is deep, but Dr. Welch is not thinking of that. He is thinking of two children who are very ill with diphtheria (dif•THEER•ee•uh). Diphtheria is a disease that people can catch from those who have it. It is a disease that kills—and kills fast.

Dr. Welch is afraid for the two children. He is also afraid for Nome. Unless he can get the right medicine, all of Nome may be wiped out. The medicine Dr. Welch needs is 1,000 miles away in Anchorage. The obstacles to transporting it are incredible. Boats and planes are of no use in this wind and snow. Nome will have to save itself in this emergency. But how?

All of Nome may be wiped out.

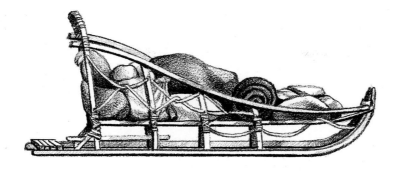

At a meeting, Dr. Welch explains the emergency. A plan is made to transport the medicine to Nome from the medical headquarters in Anchorage. Dogsledding champions—20 in all—will bring it. They and their huskies will follow the mail route, the Iditarod Trail.

Some people think it will take two weeks to sled this route, but these mushers are champions. They say they can do it in less than a week. They plan to sled without stopping.

A train takes the medicine to Nenana, 674 miles from Nome, where the trail begins. There Bill Shannon straps the box to his sled and yells "Mush!" to his huskies. The race to save Nome is on.

Edgar Kalland is waiting 50 miles away. When Shannon arrives, Kalland puts the box on his sled and takes off. Day after day, the medicine travels nonstop, passing from one musher to the next.

Iditarod Trail

❄ Then a snowstorm hits. The huskies can't keep pace. They step out of their positions and tangle their lines. The mushers must unknot the lines with freezing hands. There are no extra dog handlers along to help—not in this race. The mushers must do their best alone. They must overcome such obstacles and keep going. They dare not stop.

Almost five days have passed. Musher Gunnar Kaasen has the medicine on his sled. Kaasen and his huskies have covered 50 freezing miles, but Nome is still 3 miles away. Will they make it?

In the early morning darkness, Dr. Welch hears a rap at his door. There stands Gunnar Kaasen with a bundle. He unknots the string and hands Dr. Welch a box. The race for life has been won. The people of Nome are saved.

Think About It

1. Why did the medicine have to get to Nome fast? Why was the medicine taken on dogsleds?

2. Why do you think the dogsledding champions offered to help take the medicine to Nome?

3. After he rests, Gunnar Kaasen tells his friends about his part of the trip to Nome. What do you think he says? Write your ideas.

Gunnar Kaasen and his dogs have saved Nome.

Sequence

When you read a story, think about the **sequence**, or order, of story events. Words that tell about time order can help you follow the sequence of events in a story. These are some of the words that are used to signal time order:

first	next	after	before	last

This chart shows the sequence of some of the events in "Race for Life on the Iditarod Trail."

1. Dr. Welch sees two children with diphtheria.
↓
2. Dr. Welch explains the emergency to Nome's leaders.
↓
3. They plan to bring the medicine to Nome by dogsled.
↓
4. A train takes the medicine from Anchorage to Nenana.
↓
5. Bill Shannon and his huskies carry the medicine 50 miles.
↓

Think about the rest of the story events. What else happens? What is the sequence of those events?

Plan your own story about dogsledding. Think about the important events in your story and about the sequence of those events. Then make a chart to show your story plan.

FISHING FOR FOUR

by Celeste Albright   illustrated by Daniel Powers

"Get on board, kids."

Dad helped the three of us into our rowboat to go out
to our big boat. Suze and I sat on the board seat across
the back. Elinore, who is just four, sat on the floor of the
boat. Dad picked up the oars. Pull, glide. Pull, glide. The
rhythm of the oars bore us over the waves.

70

Our dad fishes for crabs. When the store has no bait for his traps, we help him catch some. Fishing isn't a chore to the four of us. We like it.

"I'm going to catch more fish than you!" Suze said. She and I like to compete.

The boat emitted a roar as it started up. Then it settled to a chug-chug rhythm.

Dad made sure our life jackets were buckled. Little Elinore
wore her harness over her life jacket's bulk. A line connects the
front of it to the boat and keeps her from falling overboard. Suze
and I are gratified that we are too big to need harnesses now.

Dad steered the boat far offshore. Then he disengaged the
motor. It emitted a snort and was still.

"How much bait do you need for tomorrow?" I asked.

Dad calculated. "If we can fill four bushel baskets, that will do it."

I dropped my line overboard. So did Suze and Elinore. We were fishing for bottom fish.

For a time, all was still. Elinore ignored her line. She was exploring a seashell inside a trap.

"Got one!" Suze yelled. Before you could blink, a big fish was flopping on the deck.

Then there was a tug on my line. I pulled it in fast. One more wiggling fish had retired from swimming!

The sleek fish resembled a little man with long whiskers. When its lips parted, I could see small white teeth. I felt bad for the poor, innocent thing. It was going to end up in a crab trap, but I had to help my dad.

Suze and I were still competing. Suze was keeping score. She calculated on her fingers. "I have four more than you!" she crowed.

I got three big ones. I needed two more to win. Dad looked gratified that our baskets were filling up.

"Time to go home," he said. It was starting to get dark.

I felt a tug. "Wait!" I said. "I've got one more."

Dad grabbed for the net. "Make that two more!" he said.

"I'm the winner!" I yelled.

"Nope," Suze said. "Look at that!" We had forgotten Elinore. Fish overflowed her basket and poured onto the deck. She wore a big, innocent grin. A bunch of fish had met their match, and so had Suze and I.

Dad rowed us to shore. Elinore fell asleep, but Suze and I watched the sun set over the sea we adore.

Think About It

1. Why does the family go out fishing? How do the three girls feel about fishing?

2. How do you think the other girls feel about Elinore getting the most fish? Why do you think that?

3. What do you think the three girls will talk about the next time they go fishing with their dad? Write what they might say.

77

RAINDROP IN THE SUN

by Deborah Akers   **illustrated by Miles Hyman**

Moro said Lani couldn't go with the men to gather abalones.

"Lani, you are a girl. How could you paddle a canoe? Also, these shells are very hard to get off a rock. You must be strong for this work."

Moro gave Lani a fierce look. Then he strode off to the canoes. There was no more to be said.

Lani was sad. She was also mad.

"I *am* strong. I could paddle a canoe. I could get the abalones off the rocks, too."

People from the tribe gathered on the shore.
Lani and her mother watched the canoes set out.
Lani looked forlorn.

Before Kalo, Lani's brother, got in his canoe,
he gave her a hug. "It's not fair, is it?"

"No! I could help you bring home more meat,"
Lani said.

"Do you think you could?" Kalo gave his sister a
hard look. Then he whispered, "Meet me over at the
entrance to the cove. I will hide you in my canoe."

Lani looked up at her mother, who gave her a slow smile. Then she nodded for Lani to go. Lani turned and ran for the cove. She got to the entrance before the canoes did.

When Kalo pulled up, Lani leaped into his canoe. She curled up on the bottom so no one could see her.

Kalo paddled hard. Then he floated the canoe into a rock shelter.

"We need to look low on the rocks for big shells. The big ones will have more meat," he said.

They came to some rocks with lots of seals perched on them. The seals sat in their lair and gorged on fish. They sunned themselves and admired their sleek coats. One big fellow, vainer than the rest, licked his fur all over.

Kalo and Lani smiled at each other and paddled on. Past the seals' lair, they discovered rocks with big abalones stuck to them. They lost no time in getting to work.

Kalo would grab a shell, and Lani would scrape it off with the paddle. Together they made a good team. They were quick workers, and before long they had a big load.

"We should be getting home now," said Kalo. "The waves are getting big."

In no time a fierce storm was upon them. They could see the other canoes coming their way. Then a gigantic wave flipped all those canoes over!

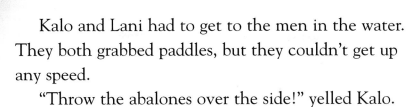

Kalo and Lani had to get to the men in the water. They both grabbed paddles, but they couldn't get up any speed.

"Throw the abalones over the side!" yelled Kalo. "They're making us too slow!"

Lani pitched all the shells but one. When they got to the canoes, Lani reached out with her paddle. She turned each one right side up. Kalo pulled Moro from the water, and the two of them helped the other men. Then they all paddled for shelter.

At last they were safe on shore. Mama and the others ran out to meet them.

Lani held out the shell she had saved. "This shell is for you, Mama. It's not much, but you can make beads from the lining."

The abalone shell was lined with mother-of-pearl. Deep inside the meat, there was something more. It was something not one of them had ever seen—an abalone pearl. Its colors shone like a raindrop in the sun.

Moro strode forward and spoke. He said the pearl was a trophy for their hero, Lani. Mama was overcome when Moro talked of how Lani and Kalo had saved the men. She was so glad to have her strong, brave girl safe at home again.

Think About It

1. Why does Moro say Lani can't go with the men to gather abalones?

2. Why do you think Kalo takes his sister along to gather abalones? How do you think he feels when the fierce storm comes up?

3. The next time the men go out to gather abalones, Lani and some other girls ask to go along. Write what you think they say and what the men tell them.

A Shaky Surprise

by Susan M. Fischer
illustrated by Janet Drew

It was Friday, the best night of the week. My friend Dave had come to sleep over, and Mom was baking us a cake. She asked us to keep an eye on Kate, my little sister.

We said we'd watch Kate, but we hoped she wouldn't get in our way. We were constructing the world's tallest stack of cards.

Dave and I are champions at stacking cards, and we often work in silence, totally engrossed in our project. This time we had to remember to watch Kate.

Kate was making a stack, too, with her blocks. Both stacks were growing taller, card by card and block by block. Ours began to get shaky, and for a moment it seemed it would fall. Then it was still, and we both grinned.

"This is our tallest stack ever!" I said to Dave.

"Mine, too," said Kate.

Then both stacks began to shake, and we heard an ominous low rumble, as if a big truck were coming. Dave and I knew what it was. "Earthquake!" we yelled.

Where we live, earthquakes can strike like a bolt of lightning. Dishes rattle, the floor creaks, and the pictures on the walls are susceptible to falling and crashing.

Now we felt the earth undulating beneath our feet, and our cards fell in a heap. Kate's blocks were heaved across the floor and wedged behind the table. Frantic, she lurched and staggered after them.

"No, Kate! Come back here!" I chased her, lurching and staggering, too.

Mom was frantic by now. "Where is Kate?" she yelled.

"She's over here, Mom! I've got her!" I said. Kate was wedged behind the table with her blocks, crying. I took her hand. "It's okay, Kate. Come with me," I told her. She nodded and got up.

Mom called, "Hurry over here to the doorway!"

A doorway is the safest part of a home in an earthquake. It's the strongest part of a wall. We all waited for the shaking to stop. It seemed to go on for a long time, but it was really only moments.

Then there was silence. It was over, and we were all okay.

"What was that big shake?" asked Kate.

"That was your first earthquake," said Mom. "Everything's fine now."

We looked around. Nothing was broken, but our stacks were in heaps. Dave and I picked up cards and blocks.

"My big stack broke," said Kate, holding up a block.

"It just fell down," I told her. "We'll help you make a new one."

Dave and I stacked Kate's blocks into a castle for her.
"You can be the queen of this castle," I told her.

"Who will be your king?" Dave asked her.

Kate smiled. "My brother," she said. "He saved me."

I smiled, too. Our fears were quickly evaporating.

Then Mom came in, grinning, with a gigantic cake.
Dave and I giggled when we saw the cake up close.
On the top, shaky frosting letters spelled out
"Happy Earthquake!"

Think About It

1. What happens when the earthquake comes? What do Mom and the children do to stay safe?

2. How can you tell that Kate's brother and his friend Dave have been in an earthquake before?

3. The next day, the friends read a newspaper story about the earthquake. Write the news story they might read.

Cause and Effect

Thinking about causes and effects can help you understand what you read. A **cause** is the reason something happens. An **effect** is what happens.

This chart shows a cause and an effect from "A Shaky Surprise."

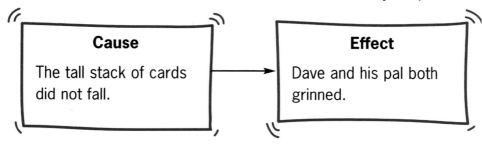

Cause

The tall stack of cards did not fall.

Effect

Dave and his pal both grinned.

One cause may have many effects, and one effect may have many causes.

Think about these effects from "A Shaky Surprise." What was the cause?

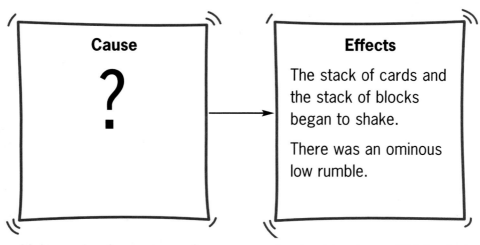

Cause

?

Effects

The stack of cards and the stack of blocks began to shake.

There was an ominous low rumble.

Make a plan for a story of your own about a big storm. Think of at least four important events for your story. Draw a cause-and-effect chart for each important event.

FLOWERS AFTER THE FLAMES

by Kana Riley   illustrated by Ed Young

The spring of 1988 started out like any other at Yellowstone National Park. Geysers spouted. Hot springs steamed. Animals roamed the forests, eating the grasses.

Then the days turned warm. Little rain fell, and the grasses turned brown. Yellowstone became as dry as tinder.

In June fires broke out. No one was surprised—fires happened every year. It was park policy to let them burn until rain showers ended them. This year, however, there were no rain showers.

Summer went by with no rain in the forecast. Fierce winds made the fires veer this way and that. Acre after acre burned.

The forest canopy went up in flames. Red-hot embers fell to the ground and started more fires. The entire region was threatened.

In late summer, fire workers dumped water and chemicals from planes. They needed to stop the fires to defend the rest of the park from the flames. By this time, however, it was too late for the water and the chemicals to help.

At last, in September, snow and rain were forecast. When they fell, they damped down the fires. The flames dwindled and finally went out.

The fires had not threatened the geysers or harmed the hot springs at Yellowstone. However, almost half of the park was blackened. It would take a long time to look the same again.

As the land renewed itself, surprising changes happened. Animals and plants found new ways to survive.

The animals' first need was for food. In the beginning the elk licked the ash for minerals. Then, in just two or three days, grass began to spring up. The elk nibbled it eagerly.

The heat of the fires had popped open the cones of tall pine trees. The seeds that spilled onto the ground fed birds and small animals.

Through the winter the land did not offer a lot to eat. Many animals, however, found enough to keep alive.

Then spring came again, and the snow melted. With each warming day, new life returned to the region.

Water trickled down into the scorched, black ground. There it soaked the hidden seeds, helping them sprout.

Spring breezes scattered seeds from plants and trees that had not burned. They, too, began to grow.

Before long, bison gathered to feed on sweet grasses. Brown bears gobbled berries from new green bushes.

Where trees used to shade the ground, the sun now shone. Flowers burst open everywhere. Acres of yellow and pink blossoms filled the new grasslands.

The sounds of birds filled the blackened forest. Woodpeckers pounded holes in burned trees to look for insects. Other birds sang from charred treetops to defend their new territories.

On the forest floor, new little pine trees sprouted. In 40 more years, they would form another forest of tall pines.

The fires had done their job. Their flames had made way for renewed life at Yellowstone.

Think About It

1. What good came of the forest fires in Yellowstone?

2. How do you think the people around Yellowstone felt about the fires in the summer of 1988?

3. You visit Yellowstone Park the summer after the forest fires and send a postcard to a friend. Write what you might tell your friend.

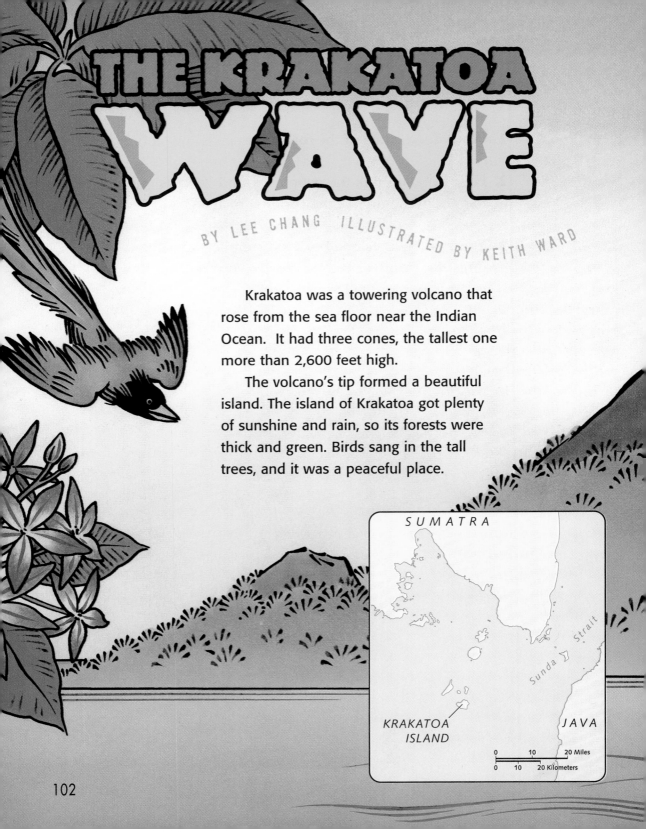

THE KRAKATOA WAVE

BY LEE CHANG ILLUSTRATED BY KEITH WARD

Krakatoa was a towering volcano that rose from the sea floor near the Indian Ocean. It had three cones, the tallest one more than 2,600 feet high.

The volcano's tip formed a beautiful island. The island of Krakatoa got plenty of sunshine and rain, so its forests were thick and green. Birds sang in the tall trees, and it was a peaceful place.

SUMATRA

KRAKATOA ISLAND

JAVA

Sunda Strait

| 0 | 10 | 20 Miles |
| 0 | 10 | 20 Kilometers |

In May of 1883, sailors on passing ships saw smoke and ash rising from the top of Krakatoa.

People in Java and Sumatra watched from their coastlines. They saw the smoke, and they could hear small explosions, too. They didn't worry about this. For years, the volcano had just groaned a little and fallen asleep again.

Everything changed on Sunday, August 26, 1883. Krakatoa woke up, this time for good!

A fierce explosion rocked the island, and the ground began to shake with earthquakes. Steam, smoke, and hot ash shot 17 miles into the sky! The ash formed such dark clouds that daytime turned to night.

The ocean began to rise and fall in a crazy way, smashing the boats in the inlet.

Then a gigantic wave rushed from the island to the shores of Sumatra and Java. Earthquakes underwater had generated a tsunami!

The tsunami wasn't like an ordinary high wave. It didn't come from the tidal bulge made by the gravitational pull of the moon. It was powered by the energy of the earthquakes started by the explosion.

The tsunami hit the coastlines hard. Frantic people ran from its path. They rushed to high ground where they might find shelter. They wished the volcano would go back to sleep, but the red glow over Krakatoa got brighter and brighter.

The next morning, great explosions began to pound the air. Krakatoa was blowing apart! The biggest blast could be heard 2,500 miles away. Later, it was said to be the loudest sound ever made on Earth.

Without warning, a new tsunami rushed over the ocean with amazing speed. The wave got bigger and bigger as it crossed the shallow waters near the coastlines. Now it was a monster wave, more than 120 feet high!

The tsunami hit the shores of Java and Sumatra with staggering might. It wiped out 165 towns. More than 36,000 people died. Not a house, not a tree, not a person was left.

The mighty wave went far around the world. It traveled 3,800 miles across the ocean in just 12 hours. (A ship would have taken 12 days!)

More than 100 years have passed, and other tsunamis have come and gone. There will be more in the years to come, but Krakatoa's wave will never be forgotten.

Think About It

1. What is a tsunami? What happened when the Krakatoa tsunami hit Java and Sumatra?

2. Why do you think Krakatoa's wave will not be forgotten?

3. Think about how Krakatoa's island looked before and after the volcano woke up. Write two lists of words and word groups to describe the island. Use your lists to write a paragraph about the island before and after Krakatoa exploded.

Graphic Sources

Stories may include maps, diagrams, schedules, graphs, charts, and tables. These are **graphic sources** that can help you understand the information in the story.

Look at this map from "The Krakatoa Wave." How does it help you understand the story?

Now look at this graph. What does it tell about the speed of the wave and the speed of a ship? How does the graph help you understand the information given in the story?

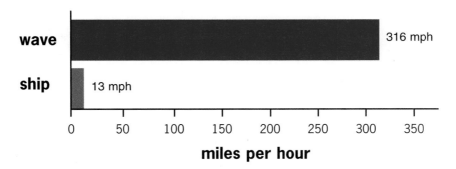

With a partner, find out about other volcanoes. Together, create a graph comparing the heights of the volcanoes.

Cindy "Science" Spots

by Mary Wright   illustrated by Debra Spina-Dixon

Cindy "Science" Vincent rode her bicycle to her friend Cyrus's house. It was icy cold out, but she didn't feel it. She was excited about her new computer and couldn't wait to tell Cyrus about it. She planned to use it to do her space research on the Internet.

Cindy parked her bicycle by the fence and rang the doorbell. When Cyrus opened the door, he was already talking excitedly. "Cindy, there's a man here you've got to meet! My dad might give him a job at the lab where he works."

the Clues

"I came over to tell you about my new computer," Cindy began. "I found a Web site for my research on plant cells in space. The experts there say . . ."

"This man was a real cosmonaut!" Cyrus broke in. "He orbited the sun with our astronauts and . . ."

"He orbited the sun? I don't think so! No one's ever done that."

"Maybe it was a star or something. Anyway, come and meet him."

111

Inside, Cindy met Professor Durak, standing in the center of the family room. "Pleased to meet you, Cindy," he said. "I was just talking about the breakthrough I made for space science back in 1969."

Cyrus's dad smiled. "Cindy is an expert on space science, Professor Durak. She plans to make it her career."

"She enrolls in Space Camp every summer," Cyrus put in.

John Glenn Neil Armstrong
Buzz Aldrin
Thanks for all your help, Prof. July, 1999

Professor Durak gave Cindy a sharp look. "The experts disregarded my formulas in planning our flight. I had to teach things to the astronauts during the launch itself! They were so grateful, they signed this shirt for me right after the flight."

"What happened with the launch?" Cyrus asked.

"The spacecraft didn't take off properly," said Professor Durak. "The astronauts had no idea what to do, but of course I did.

"Our craft rose very quickly

through the atmosphere. The altimeter numbers went up faster
and faster. We passed a satellite on our way up. Once we had
left Earth's atmosphere, ah, that was a sight to see."

"What was?" Cindy asked.

"Seeing the planets from space, of course. Mars, the red
planet. Jupiter, with its ring. Venus, with its Great Red Spot.
Now, that was something!"

"Cyrus," Cindy broke in. "Can I get something to eat? Maybe some cereal or a slice of pie?"

Cyrus frowned, but Cindy dragged him into the kitchen anyway. "Professor Durak is a fake, Cyrus!" she said. "I hope your father hasn't given him a job."

Cyrus sighed dejectedly. "You always know what you're talking about, Cindy, so you're probably right. But how do you know Professor Durak's a fake?"

115

"There are two clues. First, look closely at the professor's shirt. Next, read about Jupiter."

Can YOU spot Professor Durak's mistakes? Look at the date on his shirt. Then check out Jupiter in a book or online.

> Answer: The professor said his flight was in 1969, but the date on his shirt is 1999. The Great Red Spot is on Jupiter. It's an immense hurricane that was first seen in 1664. John Glenn, Neil Armstrong, and Buzz Aldrin were never on a mission together.

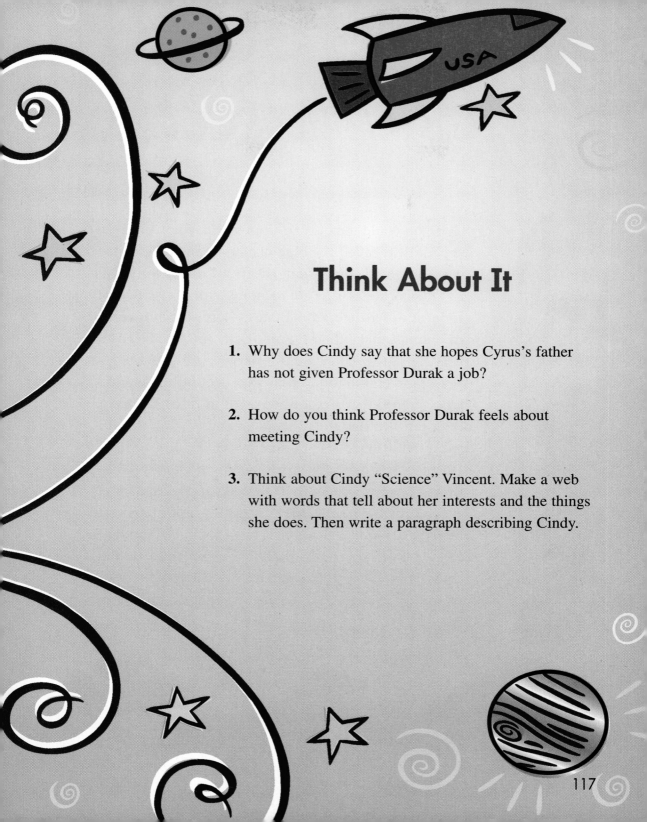

Think About It

1. Why does Cindy say that she hopes Cyrus's father has not given Professor Durak a job?

2. How do you think Professor Durak feels about meeting Cindy?

3. Think about Cindy "Science" Vincent. Make a web with words that tell about her interests and the things she does. Then write a paragraph describing Cindy.

GARDENS OF THE SEA:
Coral Reefs

by Caren B. Stelson   illustrated by James Noel Smith

If you could look down from space, you would see why Earth is called the blue planet. As the blue parts of a globe show, more than two-thirds of Earth is water.

The world's oceans are teeming with life, with the warmest waters being the richest. Here vast numbers of sea animals make their homes. Here, too, the beautiful coral reefs grow. They are the gardens of the sea.

Coral reefs are found in oceans around the world, but only in the warmest waters. For most corals, the water must be between 75 and 85 degrees—almost like bathwater. It must also be shallow, clean, and clear.

The corals that make up a reef don't grow well below 130 feet. Deeper than that, it's too cold, dark, and still for them. They need sunshine, and they need the flow of the waves to bring their food to them. Each little tube-shaped coral animal has a mouth surrounded by fingerlike sensors. These tentacles catch tiny swimming animals in the gently flowing water.

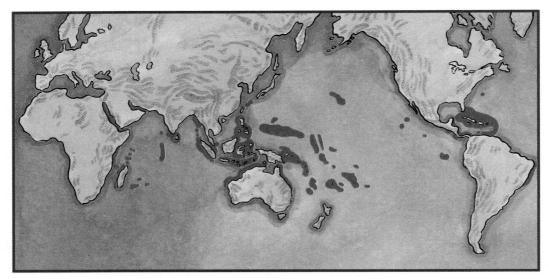

Coral reefs are found in oceans around the world.

Huge coral reefs like underwater cliffs are made by tiny animals less than $\frac{1}{2}$ inch across. How do they do it?

Each little coral animal attaches itself to the skeletons of those that lived before it. As it grows, it takes calcium from the water and uses it to form a limestone skeleton. When it dies, its hard skeleton remains. Then a new coral animal attaches on top of it. Over time, these very tiny limestone skeletons form a large coral wall. A coral reef grows very slowly—its ridges may be only 3 feet higher in 1,000 years.

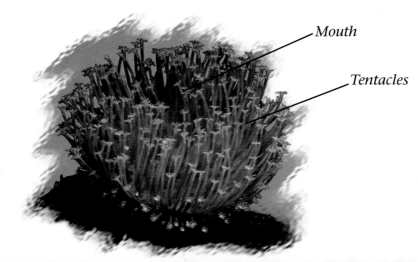

Mouth

Tentacles

CORAL

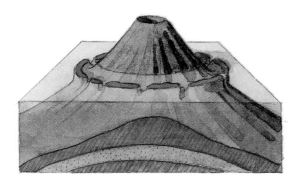

There are three kinds of reefs. A reef may grow around the edge of a volcanic island like fringe around a tablecloth. This is called a **fringing reef**. Most volcanic islands are ancient. Lava no longer flows from their craters.

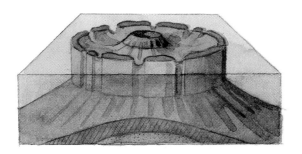

Over the years, the ocean floor may move, and the volcano may begin to sink. Water flows between the volcano and the reef, making a calm lagoon. Now the reef is called a **barrier reef**.

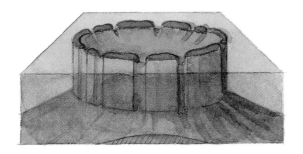

Finally the ancient volcano—crater, lava, and all—disappears. When the island slips under the water, only the reef can be seen. The ring it forms is a **coral atoll**.

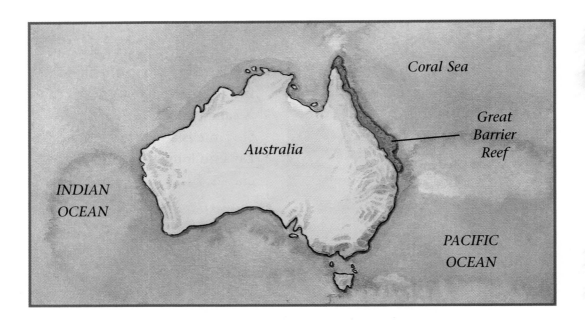

Find the Great Barrier Reef on a map or a globe. Like the Great Wall of China, it is large enough to be seen from space. No other reef is as rich with sea life as this one, the largest on Earth. Rare and colorful sea animals meander in and out of its coral gardens. Scuba divers love to visit this incredible reef to observe and photograph its strange and beautiful sea life. Here are some animals that make their homes in these warm waters.

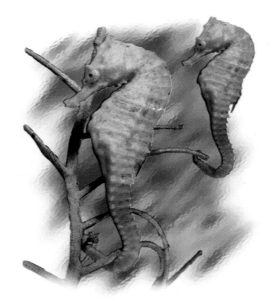

Sea Horse
Sea horses, like monkeys, have tails that can cling to plants. The males have a pouch in which they carry the eggs until they hatch. The babies use their "monkey tails" to cling together!

Longnose Butterfly Fish
These brightly colored fish have long snouts that they use to pluck food from the coral. At night they darken their bodies and sleep in coral caves.

Green Sea Turtle
These huge turtles grow to be 300 pounds and may have 4-foot-long shells. Only the female ever comes ashore. Each year she digs a hole in the sand and lays about 100 eggs.

Giant Clam
The giant clam has the biggest shell on Earth. At almost $\frac{1}{4}$ ton, it is also the largest animal without a backbone.

Crown-of-Thorns Sea Star
This big starfish feeds on coral. There are many more of them lately, so more damage is being done to the reefs.

Coral reefs are the gardens of the ocean. Clean, warm, gently moving water and sunlight keep them growing. Without these things, coral life will die, and the reefs will become barren piles of rock. Today, many coral reefs are threatened by pollution. They no longer have the clean water they need to grow in. To save the reefs, we will have to fight pollution. We must care for and preserve our beautiful gardens of the sea.

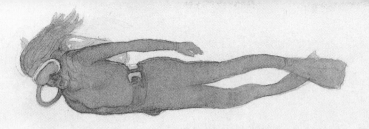

Think About It

1. Where do coral reefs grow?

2. How is a coral reef like a garden? How is it different from a garden?

3. Suppose you've been asked to write a report about one of the animals that live in the warm waters near a reef. Which animal would you choose? Write a paragraph about why you would choose that animal.

Peppermint-Peanut-Butter Fudge

by Pam Zollman

illustrated by Krieg Barrie

From our perch on the porch steps, Pearl and I could see all over the old homestead. Granny's birthday party looked like a county fair! All the relatives had gathered here for the occasion.

There would be sack races, three-legged races, and a baking contest—followed by the popular pie-eating contest! We planned to pack a lot of fun into the weekend. My sister and I should have been enjoying this happy occasion, but we weren't. We had no gift for Granny.

"Roy, I know!" said Pearl. "Let's make a tasty pan of fudge for her."

"Good choice, but you're looking at a boy who can't even boil water," I said.

Pearl said, "I'll show you how." In the kitchen, she put generous amounts of cocoa and other things into a pot. "You've been appointed to stir," she said. "Add some butter." I stirred in an entire jar of peanut butter.

Pearl was annoyed. I shrugged. "It's the same as butter, right?" I said.

"No!" replied Pearl loudly. "Oh, well—too late now." After the fudge mix boiled, she poured it into a pan.

As I stepped forward to see the result, Granny's cat ran in front of my feet. I jumped back, and my arm bumped the candy bowl. Yikes! Peppermints were adding themselves to the fudge mix!

For a brief moment I wanted to cry. "Surely I've spoiled it! Granny won't want peppermint-peanut-butter fudge."

"Don't despair," Pearl said in a kind voice. "It may be okay."

As soon as the fudge set, we sampled it. It was nice and moist, but I made a face. "It's too sweet. We'll have to throw it away."

"Let's go join in the contests," said Pearl. "We can feed the fudge to the pigs later."

Andy beat us in the sack race, and Sara won the pie-eating trophy. As we watched the relatives play table tennis, I brooded about one undeniable fact— we still had no gift for Granny.

Later, we watched Granny judge the kitchen contest. She tasted corn relish, baked beans, and meatloaf. Then she lifted the foil off a pan and tasted something I recognized—it was our fudge!

I waited for Granny to make a terrible face, but she didn't. She made a face of pure bliss! "When I was a girl," she said, "our sugar ration was precious. We used very little of it for sweets, so I really enjoy them now." She pointed to our pan. "Who concocted this wondrous fudge?"

Pearl and I raised our hands. Beaming, Granny announced, "Pearl and Roy are the kitchen champions!"

"Happy Birthday, Granny," I said. "The fudge is your gift from us." I poured her a generous glass of milk. I had a feeling she'd need it!

Granny hugged us. "You two are my best gift, more precious than the most wondrous sweets!"

I winked at Pearl. "And we were worried about the fudge."

Pearl just grinned.

Think About It

1. Why don't Roy and Pearl like the fudge they made? Why does Granny like the fudge?

2. How do you think Roy and Pearl feel when they see Granny tasting their fudge? Why?

3. After her birthday party, Granny sends Roy and Pearl a thank-you letter. Write the thank-you letter she sends.

Narrative Elements: Plot, Character, Setting

A story has three narrative elements: characters, setting, and plot.
The **characters** are the people or animals in the story.
The **setting** is the time and place in which a story happens.
The **plot** is all the story events in order.
This chart shows the narrative elements in "Peppermint-Peanut-Butter Fudge."

Characters	**Setting**
Roy	now
Pearl	the family's old homestead
Granny	

Plot
Roy and Pearl have no gift for Granny's birthday.
They make fudge for her.
Things go wrong, and the fudge is much too sweet.
Granny loves the too-sweet fudge.

Which narrative element would change if Pearl were not at the birthday party for Granny? Which narrative element would change if Granny agreed with Roy and Pearl that the fudge was much too sweet?

Plan your own story about a party. Think about the narrative elements you want to use. Then draw a chart like the one above to show your story plan.

133

AWESOME ANTS

by Lisa Eisenberg • illustrated by John Berg

January 14

Lawton and Company:

Our class saw your ad for ant farms in *Animals: Jaws, Paws, and Claws.* We have raised enough money to get a farm for our classroom. We would like to order Item 1036-A, the Deluxe Ant Farm with 48 average-sized ants. We are sending you a check to cover the cost.

Thank you,
Fifth Grade,
Paulson School

January 20

Fifth Grade,
Paulson School:

Thank you for your order. Interest in ants is booming! The big demand for ant farms has caused some small delays in shipping. As soon as your ants become available, they will be shipped to you.

Best wishes,
Lawton and Company

February 20

Lawton and Company:

We are distressed about the delay in our order. This is very awkward for us. We want to have our ants soon. When will they be available?

Fifth Grade,
Paulson School

March 1

Fifth Grade,
Paulson School:

We regret your disappointment. We are negotiating with a new distributor because the one we had was inefficient. Your ants will arrive soon!

Happy farming,
Lawton and Company

March 10

Lawton and Company:

Once again, we are forced to complain. The ant farm we ordered was supposed to include 48 *average*-sized ants. The ants you shipped us are *gigantic*! Some are more than an inch long! They do not even fit into the ant farm. Please send us the right ants without delay.

Thank you,
Fifth Grade,
Paulson School

April 1

Fifth Grade,
Paulson School:

We are sorry to hear of your disappointment with your order. Our new distributor specializes in lab ants. They sent you Dinoponera grandis ants, ordered for a lab, by mistake. A duplicate shipment, this time with average-sized ants, is on the way. Please keep the Dinoponera grandis ants as a gift from us!

Best wishes,
Lawton and Company

Lawton and Company: April 10

We now know why you wanted us to keep
the *Dinoponera grandis* ants. Their appetites
are awesome! It was awful to see them eat the
principal's straw hat. We were forced to get her
a new one. We're sending the bill for it to the
distributor who specializes in lab ants. We're
sending YOU something, too—the ants!

                     Sincerely,
                     Fifth Grade,
                     Paulson School

Bill

One straw
hat !

$35.00

Lawton and Company Memo

TO: All Departments
FROM: Mail Room

ALERT:
A shipment of Dinoponera grandis ants has been returned by a class at Paulson School. The ants ate their way out of the shipping box, and we haven't caught them all. There is no cause for alarm. The ants are large, but they are friendly, and

Think About It

1. Why does the Fifth Grade at Paulson School complain to Lawton and Company?

2. How do you think the Paulson School fifth graders would feel if they knew that the gigantic ants had eaten their way out of the shipping box?

3. The fifth graders' teacher asks them to write a paragraph explaining what they learned from their ant farm project. Write a paragraph that one of the students would write.

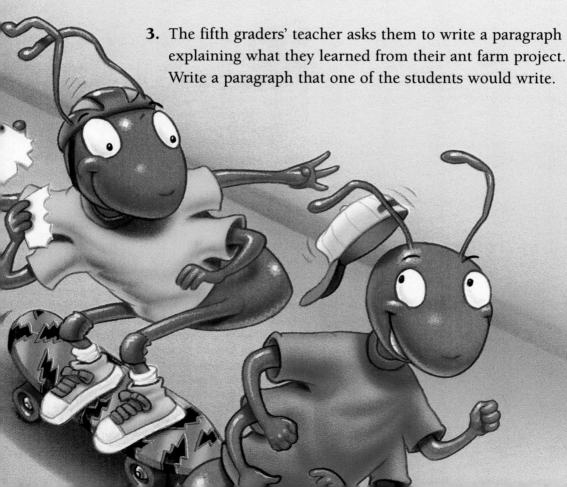

141

MY IMAGINARY WORLD

WRITTEN AND ILLUSTRATED BY ISTVAN BANYAI

How did I become an illustrator? It started like this. When I was a boy growing up in Hungary, people didn't have TVs in their homes. We did lots of other things for fun. I rode my bicycle almost every day. Sometimes I would cross one of the seven bridges spanning the Danube River and ride into downtown Budapest.

I had no brothers or sisters, so I often played alone. Perhaps that is why I dreamed up such a vivid imaginary world.

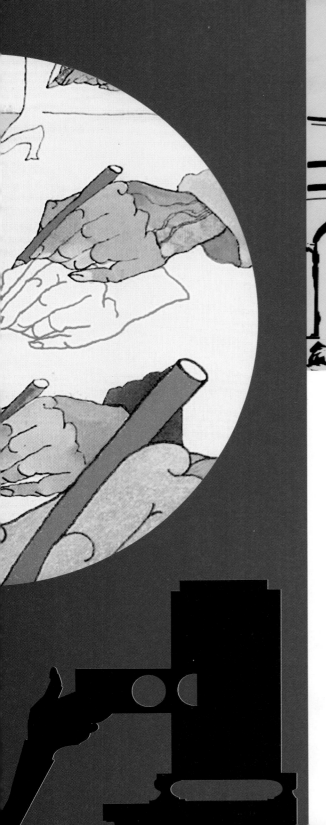

My mother died when I was born, so my grandmother raised me. She had so many wonderful old things in her house. There were wooden boxes full of old photos, ancient maps, and other mementos of times past.

Of all my grandmother's old things, her slide lantern was my favorite. She would let me put the beautiful hand-painted glass slides into it myself. Then the light inside it would flash their images onto my wall.

143

When I was a child, I spent much time drawing. I had a good teacher who encouraged me.

Like an author, I made up stories—some scary and some not—as I sketched. Sometimes I invented entire armies to battle each other in my sketches. These drawings were scary, but others were funny and made people laugh. Using my pencil, I could enter my imaginary world anytime I wanted.

Istvan Banyai

Later, I went to art classes. I learned about many different styles and experimented with using charcoal and pastels. However, I found that using a pencil was still my favorite way to draw. Now I've developed a style of my own, but I always begin my work in pencil.

First, I make a series of drawings. Then I transfer them to clear plastic sheets. Finally, I paint bright colors inside the lines on the back of the plastic. The pictures I did for the book *Zoom* took me more than 120 hours to complete!

Illustrating is my job. I wake up every morning and take a shower in ideas. I burn my toast, and the crumbs on the counter remind me of the dots my pencil makes. Sometimes I start the sketches for a new book by making dots and then staring at them. Before long, they begin to look like something—perhaps tiny planets floating in space.

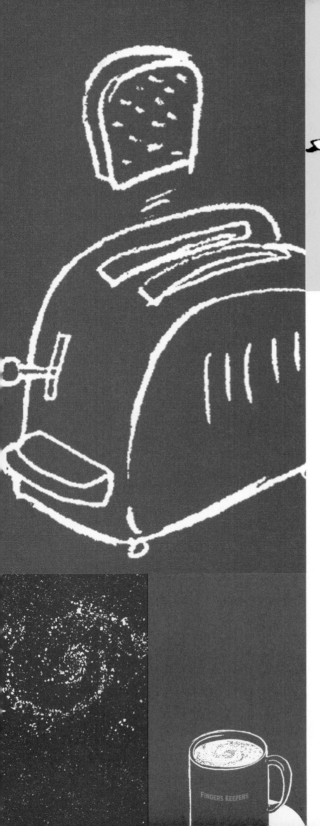

Suddenly I leave behind the mess in the kitchen. I move from the real world to a wondrous imaginary place. Here no one ever burns the toast, and the sun shines down on a morning that never ends.

I am the author of my own stories. I make up the characters and give them things to do. I draw the house where they live. The books I illustrate are windows into my imaginary world—a place you are always welcome to visit.

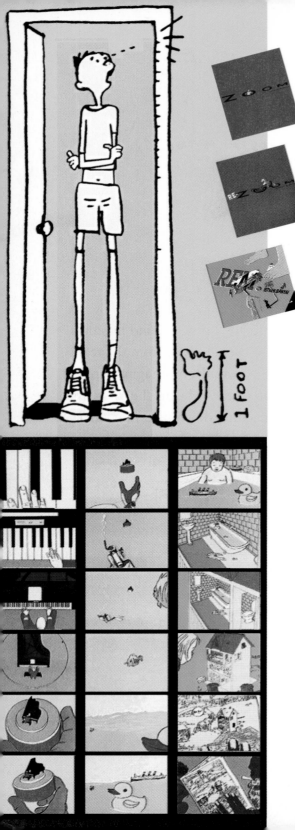

Books by Istvan Banyai:

Zoom
Re-Zoom
REM (Rapid Eye Movement)
by Istvan Banyai
(Viking/Penguin)

Poems for Children Nowhere Near Old Enough to Vote
by Carl Sandburg
illustrated by Istvan Banyai
(Knopf)

Think About It

1. Which parts of Istvan Banyai's childhood helped him become an illustrator?

2. How does Istvan Banyai feel about his work as an illustrator? How can you tell?

3. If you had a chance to meet Istvan Banyai, what else would you want to know about him and his work? Write at least four questions you would ask him.

Fact and Opinion

Thinking about facts and opinions can help you understand what you read.

A **fact** is a statement that can be proved.

This drawing was done in charcoal.

An **opinion** is someone's belief about something. An opinion cannot be proved.

It's the best drawing I've ever done.

Read the sentences in the box. Which sentences are facts? Which are opinions? How can you tell?

Artists work in many different styles.

A pencil is the best tool for drawing.

These pastel drawings are beautiful.

This off-white paper is heavier than that white paper.

Look at each picture and write two sentences about what you see. Make your first sentence a fact. Make your second sentence an opinion.

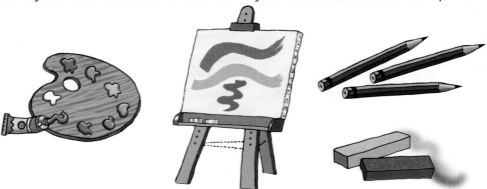

WITH LOVE FROM *Ella*

by Susan M. Fischer
illustrated by Stan Shaw

**An Imaginary Letter
from Ella Fitzgerald to a Fan**

January 28, 1992

Dear Drew,

Thank you for your nice letter. I had to pause to smile when you called me your hero. You flatter me! I think it's grand that you want to be a composer. So, you want to know about my career? I'll be glad to tell you a little about my life.

I was born in 1918, yet I am much like you, Drew. We both adore music and have been surrounded by it from an early age.

150

My childhood was a happy one. My mother and I lived in New York near a pawnshop and a produce market. From the time I was a little girl, I loved to sing at church. I also sang with my friends on our front stoop in the afternoons after school. Soon I could imitate the styles of singers who were familiar from the radio. Some of their voices were smooth, and some were gravelly. I had good pitch—I could sing each note in perfect tune. However, what I really loved to do was dance.

151

The truth is, I wanted to be a dancer when I grew up. When I was sixteen, something happened to change that. I was out running errands with my friends, and they dared me to dance at a contest. I agreed to do it and took the trolley to the Harlem Opera House. On the stage, however, I froze. My feet simply would not move, and I *had* to do some sort of act or look like a fool. So I sang! That night I won first prize. I knew then that singing was the career for me.

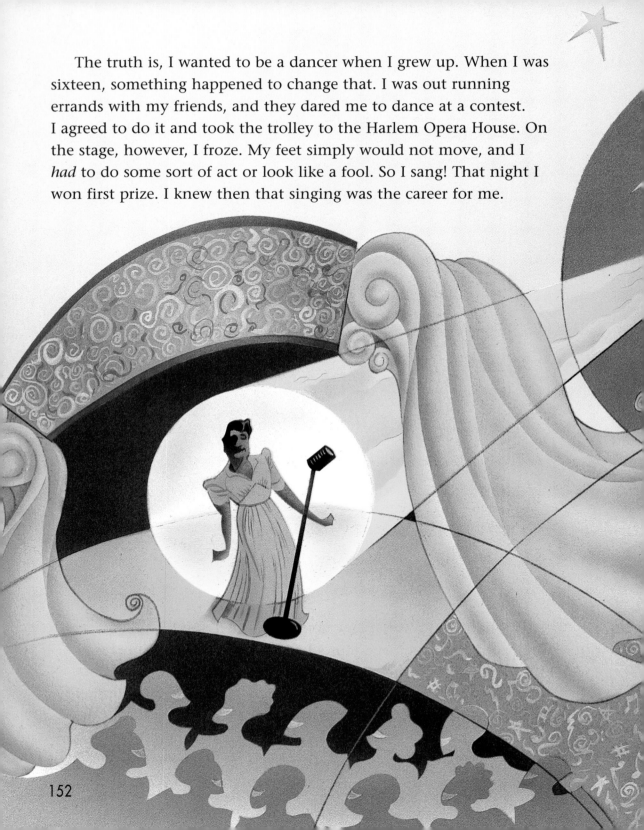

My confidence grew, and I competed in more contests and won them all. One night a familiar-looking man came to hear me sing. He was Chick Webb, the leader of a jazz band and a well-known figure in the music industry. He liked what he heard and hired me to sing with his band! He helped me develop a style and rhythm all my own. I rehearsed every day. Chick introduced me to numerous people important in the industry, and this gave my career a boost. I was becoming an international star.

Chick was also a composer, and together we wrote numerous songs. In 1938, I recorded one of them. It was called "A-Tisket, A-Tasket." It sold a million copies in only a couple of weeks, and it is still one of my best-known songs. When Chick died, I felt so blue. I became the leader of the band, and we played our music everywhere. The public loved us, as jazz was very popular. After three years, however, I paused to consider my career. It was time for me to leave the band and go solo.

I sang all over the world. I could sing any style of music, and I invented a style of my own. I used my voice to make sounds like those of a musical instrument. This new style I called "scat" singing, and music experts loved it. The public loved it, too. It became part of jazz history. So not only is jazz a part of me— I am a part of jazz!

Be true to your dreams, Drew, and maybe one day you can compose a song for me. Thank you again for your letter.

With love from *Ella*

In her long career, Ella Fitzgerald recorded more than 200 songs and earned 13 Grammys. Some say she was the greatest singer of all time. She appeared on stage for the last time in 1993. Ella Fitzgerald died on June 15, 1996. Over the years Ella gathered numerous awards and honors. In 1995 she became a member of the National Women's Hall of Fame. The "First Lady of Song" will always be remembered for her "scat" style of jazz singing.

Think About It

1. How did Ella Fitzgerald develop her love of music?

2. Why did she become a singer instead of a dancer?

3. When Drew is asked to write a paragraph about a famous American, he chooses Ella Fitzgerald. In his paragraph, he must explain his choice. Write the paragraph Drew turns in to his teacher.

LOURDES LÓPEZ:
Ballet Star

by Doris Licameli
illustrated by Rosemary Fox

Lourdes López (LAWRD•es LOH•pez) was born in Cuba on May 2, 1958. A year later, the López family moved to Florida, where Lourdes grew up.

When Lourdes was 5, her doctor ordered special shoes to correct a problem with her feet. At the shoe store, Lourdes spied ballet shoes. While the clerk wrapped her plain, brown shoes, Lourdes wriggled her toes into the ballet shoes. *Oh, to be a ballerina!*

Soon Lourdes had a happy surprise. The doctor also ordered dance lessons to make her legs stronger. Lourdes began taking ballet classes. The teacher could see that Lourdes had real talent.

When she was 8, Lourdes began to study with Alexander Nigodoff. He introduced his students to story ballets such as *Cinderella* and *Sleeping Beauty*. He showed them the steps of dances from those ballets. Lourdes enjoyed dance more than ever!

Dancing six days a week left little time for fun. "Why do you devote so much time to ballet?" her friends asked. It made Lourdes a little sad, knowing that they didn't understand her love of dance.

SCRAP BOOK

Then Lourdes performed at a school event. As her friends watched, Lourdes demonstrated her artistic skill. When her dance ended, her friends cheered. Lourdes bowed in triumph.

Later, Lourdes won a full scholarship to the School of American Ballet. She was only 14 when she said good-bye to her family. She moved to New York City with her sister, Terry.

Lourdes took classes in ballet technique every day. She worked hard and learned fast. Very soon, George Balanchine, the school's founder, took note of Lourdes. Under his coaching, her talent bloomed.

NEW YORK SCHOOL

RECOGNIZES

Lourdes Ló

New York City Ballet's Glittering Season

BY EUCLITIWOU

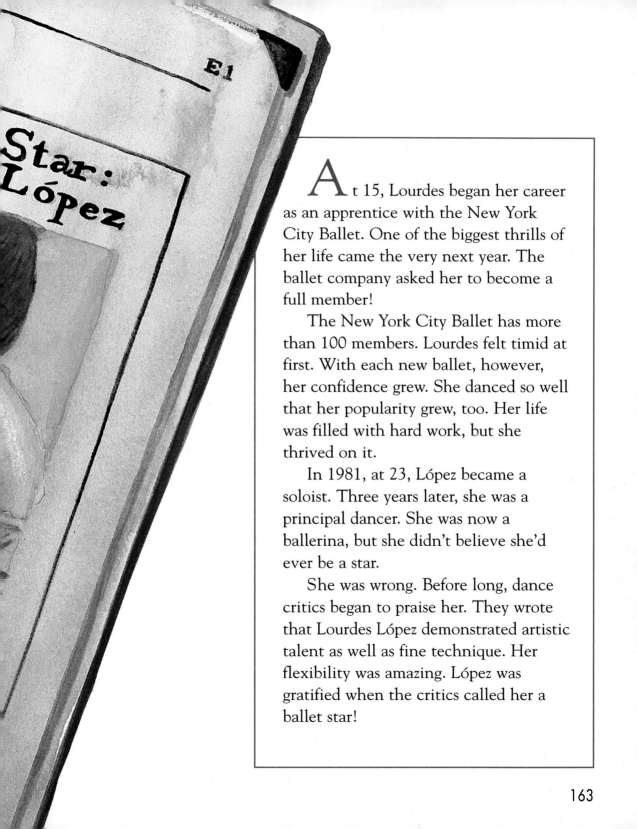

At 15, Lourdes began her career as an apprentice with the New York City Ballet. One of the biggest thrills of her life came the very next year. The ballet company asked her to become a full member!

The New York City Ballet has more than 100 members. Lourdes felt timid at first. With each new ballet, however, her confidence grew. She danced so well that her popularity grew, too. Her life was filled with hard work, but she thrived on it.

In 1981, at 23, López became a soloist. Three years later, she was a principal dancer. She was now a ballerina, but she didn't believe she'd ever be a star.

She was wrong. Before long, dance critics began to praise her. They wrote that Lourdes López demonstrated artistic talent as well as fine technique. Her flexibility was amazing. López was gratified when the critics called her a ballet star!

In 1988, Lourdes hurt her foot. She knew that this might threaten her dance career. Luckily, however, she made a fast recovery. She returned to the stage in triumph, her popularity higher than ever.

Lourdes stopped dancing with the New York City Ballet in 1997. Now she devotes her time to working with the children of New York City. Lourdes shows them what ballet can mean to their lives.

Think About It

1. How did Lourdes López's dancing career develop in New York City?

2. Do you think Lourdes López would have become a ballet star even if the doctor had not ordered dance lessons for her? Tell why you think as you do.

3. What do you think Lourdes López might have written in her diary on the day a dance critic first called her a star? Write her diary entry.

Certain Steps

by Charlene Norman
illustrated by Shelly Meridith

"Vote for Al. He's a pal!" Al said, making *V*'s for victory with his fingers. "You and I should team up on this campaign, Murphy. Then I know I'd beat Casey in the student council election."

"What's your platform?" Murphy asked.

"Maybe I'll stand on a chair when I give my speech."

Murphy shook his head. "A platform is what you plan to do if you're elected."

"My campaign comes first," Al said. "I plan to take certain steps so all the kids will know who I am."

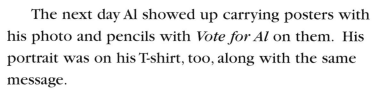

The next day Al showed up carrying posters with his photo and pencils with *Vote for Al* on them. His portrait was on his T-shirt, too, along with the same message.

"What's your platform? What do you plan to do for your fellow students?" Murphy asked as they hung posters.

Al laughed. "Cut out all homework! Here, take a bunch of these pencils. I'm going to get the crossing guard to endorse my campaign." As he left, Al made an A-Okay sign with his hand and called back, "Certain steps, easy win!"

NiCE HAT

Abraham Who?

Murphy had seldom seen his buddy act so obnoxious. He grew concerned about Al's "certain steps" and hung his posters in an uncertain mood.

A portrait of Abraham Lincoln standing in front of one of his residences caught Murphy's eye. He felt the President's gaze upon him. Was it challenging him to stand up for what was right? "I'll help Al run a good campaign," he vowed silently.

Then he noticed some graffiti on the wall, luckily just in pencil. He used one of Al's pencils to erase it. Some kids stopped to help and happily kept the pencils.

Murphy picked up trash around the playground while he waited for Al to finish his morning patrol job. Other kids noticed and joined Murphy.

On the way to class, Murphy gave Al some ideas for ways to improve things for students.

"I don't think so, Murphy," Al said. "Those ideas sound like too much work."

Murphy spoke sadly but firmly. "Al, I know those are the kind of steps a candidate should be taking." He looked down and apologized. "I'm sorry, but I just can't work on a campaign that promises no homework."

After lunch, Murphy was sitting on a bench outside, reading with a first grader. Al nodded to Murphy and then turned to whisper to several girls. They all turned to look as Al pointed to Murphy.

During geography, Murphy heard whispered phrases that included his name. Kids he considered friends stared at him and giggled. Murphy had felt certain he'd taken the right step to refuse to help Al. Now, however, the stares and whispers increased his mood of uncertainty. Should he apologize and support Al's campaign?

Later in the day the candidates gave their speeches. Casey promised Pizza Fridays. Then Al spoke.

"A student who cares a lot," he said, stretching his arms wide for emphasis, "will organize student volunteers. You can join the group of your choice to pick up trash, remove graffiti, or read with first graders once a week. Vote for the person I'm voting for. Cross off Al and write in Murphy. You'll seldom have a leader who cares as much."

Kids laughed and clapped as Murphy grinned. Al smiled and shook his hand. Then the teacher said it was time to vote.

Think About It

1. Why does Murphy finally refuse to help Al with his campaign?

2. How do you think Murphy feels when he hears other kids giggling and whispering phrases that include his name?

3. Think about the main character, Murphy. Make a web with words that tell what Murphy thinks, likes, and does. Then using your web as a plan, write a paragraph about Murphy.

Predict Outcomes

As you read a story, you may want to try to figure out what will happen next. You can use story events and your own experiences to make predictions. Not all your predictions will turn out to be right. Still, making predictions helps you think about and understand the story.

This chart shows how you might make a prediction while reading "Certain Steps."

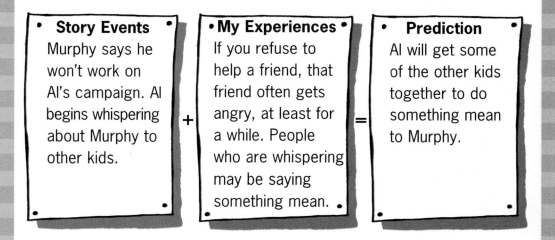

Story Events
Murphy says he won't work on Al's campaign. Al begins whispering about Murphy to other kids.

+

My Experiences
If you refuse to help a friend, that friend often gets angry, at least for a while. People who are whispering may be saying something mean.

=

Prediction
Al will get some of the other kids together to do something mean to Murphy.

Think about the prediction. Is that what you thought would happen? Is it what does happen in the story? How do you think making that prediction helped you understand the story?

Reread the ending of "Certain Steps." What do you predict will happen when the kids vote? Draw a chart to show how you make your prediction.

Story Events + **My Experiences** = **Prediction**

Quest for a Healthy World

by Carol Storment
illustrated by Josephine Hill

Jonas Salk always wanted to know everything about the world around him—his first excited words were "Dirt, dirt!" When he grew up, he planned to be a lawyer. Before long, however, Salk realized that he cared more about the laws of nature. It was a lucky day for people around the world when he switched from law school to medical school.

Jonas Salk did not intend to become a doctor who treated people, but he took all the training to do so. He really wanted to be a medical scientist.

While still a student, Salk helped work on a vaccine to prevent influenza, or flu. He was very interested in this project because he wanted to test something that one of his medical teachers had claimed. This teacher had stated that illnesses caused by bacteria could be prevented by injecting people with killed germs for those diseases. He insisted, however, that this method didn't work for illnesses, such as the flu, that are caused by viruses.

Dr. Salk at work in his lab

**1914
Jonas Edward Salk
born in New York City**

Salk suspected that a killed-virus vaccine had been tried without success. That didn't mean the method could never succeed, he reasoned. This seemed like the right time to go ahead and try it again.

Through careful experiments, Salk found that it *was* possible to use killed viruses. In time he developed a flu vaccine that has saved thousands of lives.

When Salk was a boy in New York City, the spread of flu threatened people's lives each year. Now a flu threat can be stopped in its tracks, thanks to his "flu shot."

THE NEWSPAPER

Salk

Plan a

MAGAZINE

Dr. Jonas Salk

VACCINE

1939 ──────
Received his M.D. from New York University School of Medicine

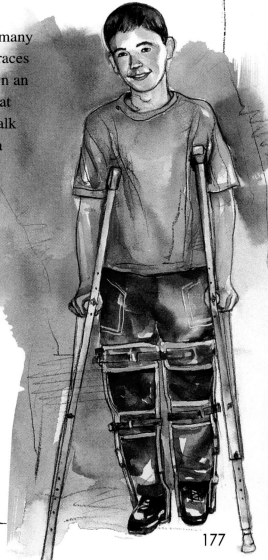

Polio was much, much worse. After it hit, many people could not walk without unwieldy leg braces and crutches. Some lived a life of immobility in an iron lung. This was a tank with an air pump that helped them breathe. Many people died. Dr. Salk knew that his next quest would be to develop a vaccine for this illness.

The research required many experiments and much time to decipher the enormous amount of data. Dr. Salk hit many dead ends, but he always looked at them as chances to learn.

After Dr. Salk's dramatic discovery, he became well known. He was astonished and dismayed by his fame. It was hard for him to keep on with his work, and that was what he wanted to do most.

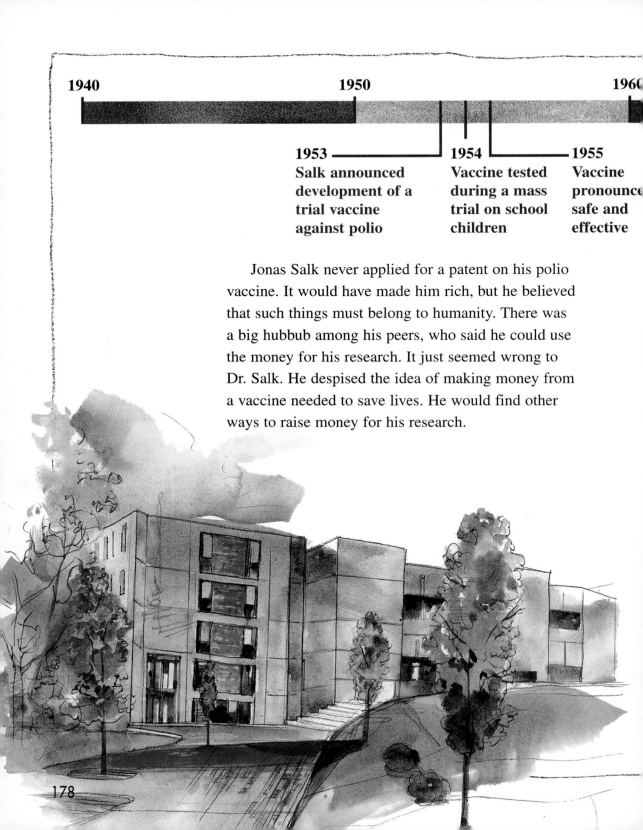

1940	1950	1960

1953 — Salk announced development of a trial vaccine against polio

1954 — Vaccine tested during a mass trial on school children

1955 — Vaccine pronounce safe and effective

Jonas Salk never applied for a patent on his polio vaccine. It would have made him rich, but he believed that such things must belong to humanity. There was a big hubbub among his peers, who said he could use the money for his research. It just seemed wrong to Dr. Salk. He despised the idea of making money from a vaccine needed to save lives. He would find other ways to raise money for his research.

Looking back on his life, Dr. Salk remembered
teachers who were important to him. Some of them were
from his early school years. He also had a favorite instructor
in medical school.

In many ways, however, he felt that his best teacher
was his mother. She came to America as a young girl
and had to work to help her family.
She did not have the chance to
go to school, but she saw to it
that her children did. She knew
what a dramatic difference it
would make to their lives. It
was Jonas Salk's mother who
started him on the path that
led to his lifesaving
achievements.

1980   1990   2000

**1995
Dr. Salk dies
at age 81**

Dr. Salk was asked what he would tell children and teenagers who were thinking about career choices. He said that each one of us has something to give to life on earth. That gift is different for everyone. The best way to have a sense of purpose is to first know ourselves. We need to know what we care about and then work for that dream.

Jonas Salk believed that it is important for us to do something that helps humanity as well as ourselves. His own quest to develop vaccines against viruses has helped the health of the entire world.

Think About It

1. What did Jonas Salk achieve in his quest for a healthy world?

2. Why do you think Jonas Salk chose to become a medical scientist rather than a doctor?

3. Think about Dr. Salk's accomplishments. Choose one or two you feel are important and write Dr. Salk a thank-you letter.

Dr. Salk

Pete's Great Invention

by Linda Lott   illustrated by Beppie Giacobbe

It was ten after eight when Pete slipped into his seat.

"Pete," Miss Deighton said with a scowl, "you are tardy again."

"He didn't want to break his streak," Mark called out. "He's been late eight days in a row now."

The class giggled, but Pete's face turned red.

"That's enough racket," Miss Deighton said. "Pete, please make an effort to be on time from now on."

It wasn't that Pete didn't care about being late. He simply couldn't seem to get up in the morning.

The loud noise of the nearby refinery starting up for the day didn't wake him. He slept soundly through the screech of the early morning freight train, too. A little alarm clock was no match for that kind of deep sleep because Pete could turn it off without ever really waking up.

When Pete was asleep, a mysterious veil seemed to muffle *all* his senses. If he took a nap after he came home, even the smell of a great steak dinner wouldn't wake him.

Pete was afraid his grades would slip if he continued to be tardy every day. What could he do?

Then Pete had an idea. Everyone had to make an original invention for the class invention fair. Why not solve two problems at once by inventing a super alarm? If his invention was a success, he would never be late again, and he would also get a good grade from Miss Deighton.

Pete wrote out a detailed description of what he planned to do. He drew and labeled a diagram. Then he set to work.

First, Pete insulated one wall of his bedroom with blankets. His alarm should not wake his grandma in the next room.

Next, he took down a hanging model plane and threaded a rope through its hook. He attached pots and pans to one end of the rope and shook them. What a racket they made!

Then Pete tied a weight to the other end of the rope and raised the pots and pans. He set the weight on top of his alarm clock's switch.

Pete's plan was that when he sleepily fumbled to turn off his alarm, he would knock over the weight. This would jerk the rope and jangle the pots and pans.

Pete's family couldn't wait to see his mysterious invention. His dad reminded him of one thing.

"Don't forget about the cat! He prowls around the house every night, and you wouldn't want him to trigger your alarm too soon."

Pete tried making a cardboard partition to fit around his bed, but the cat easily jumped over it. Oh well—he could just shut his door at night.

When Pete let his family see his invention, his mom grumbled a little about her pots and pans. Then she thought about their hectic mornings and said, "Never mind. If it works, it'll be worth it!"

A week later, Pete submitted his super alarm to the class invention fair. He set it up, read aloud the description, and demonstrated how it worked. His classmates covered their ears, but they knew a useful invention when they heard one.

"Now, that's what I call an original idea!" Mark called out. The class cheered loudly to show that they agreed with Mark. Miss Deighton agreed with Mark, too. She winked at Pete.

"I already knew your invention was a great success," she said. "You haven't been late once since you invented it!"

Think About It

1. What does Pete invent? How does Miss Deighton know that Pete's invention is a success?

2. Do you think other people would be interested in using Pete's great invention? Why or why not?

3. Pete wants to try selling his invention to other people. He writes an ad to put on some posters. Write the ad that Pete may have written.

Author's Purpose and Perspective

Thinking about the author's purpose and perspective can help you understand what you read.

An **author's purpose** is his or her reason for writing. In almost all cases, an author's purpose is to entertain readers, to inform readers, or to persuade readers.

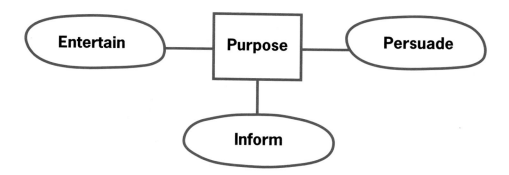

An **author's perspective** is his or her viewpoint on a subject. It includes his or her opinions and attitudes.

Think about the author's purpose in writing "Pete's Great Invention." Do you think the author wrote this story to entertain readers, to inform readers, or to persuade readers? How would the story be different if the author's purpose were to inform readers about the steps in inventing something? How would it be different if the author's purpose were to persuade readers to give Pete an award for his invention?

Plan your own paragraph about an invention you would like to create. Be sure to include your perspective, or point of view. First, choose a purpose for your paragraph. Write a sentence that states your purpose. Then make a web to show your paragraph plan. Be sure that all the parts of your plan support your purpose.

THE MYSTERY OF THE CRIMSON CARDS

BY PAM ZOLLMAN
ILLUSTRATED BY
REGAN DUNNICK

"You got a card, too, Hector?" I asked incredulously. All the red paper cards were homemade, not bought. Each had a different design, made just for the person who got it.

"Wow, Carla!" Hector said. "You ought to see this." The card he handed me had sketches of dogs on it. "Someone knows how much I love beagles," he said. Like the rest, Hector's card wasn't signed.

"Yen," I called to the girl in the back of the class, "did you get a card?"

Yen shook her head stolidly as if she didn't care. I bet she wants one as much as I do, I thought.

"Jake, what about you?" Hector asked our classmate in the jaunty clothes.

"Not yet," Jake replied, smiling.

"Tim, did you get one?" I asked. He was drawing a volcano.

"Nope," he said, as he added more lava to his art.

"Tim's artistic," I pointed out to Hector. "His art was in a school exhibition once, so maybe he's the mystery artist."

Hector shrugged. "You could be right. I think Mrs. Benson is doing it, though."

Just then Mrs. Benson said, "This card is exquisite! It looks like the modern art I decorate my house with." Torn colored paper was arranged in abstract designs on her card.

"Now," I said, "the only people who haven't gotten a card yet are Yen, Tim, Jake . . . and me." Impulsively I added, "Tomorrow I'll hide and catch the card person."

"I'll help you," Hector said.

We thought we had a perfect plan. The next day we hid behind some cabinets. We saw something, but it wasn't the card person. We saw Tim's books slide through his arms, as if of their own accord. Jake, passing by, fell over the books, causing a dramatic hubbub.

Then Hector pointed. "You and Jake have cards on your desks!"

In my rush, I bumped into Yen. "Sorry," I apologized.

I noticed Yen hesitate before she gave me a timid smile. She was always so quiet and shy.

Jake held up his card. A picture of his favorite singer was pasted to crimson paper, surrounded by musical notes.

Watercolor roses decorated my card. They made me smile because I love roses. They are my favorite flower. I thought about how thorough the card person was, and whoever it was had been thoughtful enough to learn something about each of us.

My suspicions returned to Tim, who was busy drawing again. I told Hector, "Tim's the card person. He can draw and he doesn't have a card yet. I'm sure the card person wouldn't give himself a card."

"That's right," said Hector. "I bet he dropped his books on purpose to distract us. That was when he gave cards to you and Jake."

Hector and I thought our reasoning skills worthy of real detectives. The next day we kept out of sight once again to catch Tim.

What a disappointment! Although we didn't see anyone, both Timmy and Yen held up crimson cards.

Mrs. Benson asked, "Who made these cards? They're worthy of an exhibition for the entire school."

I saw Yen hesitate before she raised her hand. "I heard you all talking about your favorite things, so I thought I'd make cards just for you."

"Thanks, Yen" I said. "Now it's our turn to find out about you."

Yen's smile wasn't timid any more.

Think About It

1. Who makes the crimson cards? Why does she make them?

2. How do her classmates feel about the crimson cards?

3. If she made a crimson card for you, what would be drawn on it? Create your card, using a sketch of the decorations and a message to describe them.

197

One of a Kind

by Ann W. Phillips   illustrated by Patrick Joseph O'Malley

What Jenna liked best about school was Friday afternoons. That was when Mr. Lee would say, "Time for the widget game!"

The widget was whatever object Mr. Lee was thinking of. Teams would ask questions to help them identify the widget. The winners got points added to their column on the board—points that counted toward a pizza party. The pizza was bait, Jenna knew, but it was good bait.

Some kids thought the game was dumb, but Jenna didn't think so. To Jenna, it was like a mystery, and she saw herself as a word detective on assignment.

Andy's team didn't think the game was dumb, either. They had vowed they'd beat Jenna's team.

Jenna's team was ahead, but not by much. They had to win—their reputation and their honor were at stake. They would let nothing sidetrack them. Jenna and Peter and Holly had taken a solemn oath: "Pizza or bust!"

"Here's your first clue," said Mr. Lee. "The widget doesn't whistle. Questions?"

The teams took turns asking questions. This time Andy's team went first. Jenna leaned forward and squinted in serious concentration. When a team felt ready to guess what the widget was, someone would blow his or her kazoo. You had to be pretty certain, though. If you guessed wrong, your team was out of the game.

"Is it smaller than the room?" Andy asked.

"Yes."

Jenna chewed her thumb and listened to the answers with complete concentration.

"Is it bigger than a book?"

"Yes."

"Can you comb your hair with it?" That was Colin's team—they were never serious. They got a *no*.

"Does it have hair?" A few laughs—and a *no*.

The questions flew. "Is it something you read?" Another *no*.

"Can you eat it for lunch?" *No* again.

At last it was Jenna's team's turn, and Peter asked an important question.

"Is it one of a kind, or are there lots of them?"

"One of a kind," said Mr. Lee with a big grin. "Definitely one of a kind."

Bingo! Like a flash of light, the answer came to Jenna, and she grabbed for her kazoo. It rolled off her desk into the aisle. Out of the corner of her eye, she could see Andy reaching for his kazoo. There was no time to check with the rest of her team. Jenna dove into the aisle, snatched up her kazoo, and blew it.

"Jenna," Mr. Lee said, "would you like to identify the widget, or are you just rolling in the aisle?"

Everyone laughed as Jenna scrambled to her feet. What if she was wrong and her guess was dumb? There would go the pizza party for everyone. Squinting at the floor, she became absorbed in staring at the toes of her shoes. Her brain was numb.

"We're listening, Jenna," prompted Mr. Lee.

Jenna took a deep breath, looked up at the teacher, and pointed. "You," she said at last. "You are the widget, Mr. Lee."

"Correct!" Mr. Lee said, beaming at her. "I can't whistle, and I'm smaller than the room but bigger than a book. You can't comb your hair with me, read me, or eat me for lunch. Furthermore, I don't have hair—well, not much!" He grinned as the kids giggled. "I am definitely one of a kind."

"Pizza! Pizza! Pizza!" Jenna's team cheered. "Hooray for Jenna!"

Jenna was beaming, too. Another widget assignment successfully completed by a winning word detective!

Think About It

1. How does Jenna figure out that Mr. Lee is the widget?

2. How does Jenna feel just before she gives her answer?
   How does she feel right after she gives her answer?

3. Write a sentence telling what classroom object you would
   choose if you were the leader in the widget game. Then write
   five questions you would ask to help identify a widget.

A Safe Harbor

by Susan McCloskey

illustrated by David Christiana

My name is Manolo Sánchez (MAH•noh•loh SAHN•chez), and as a child I lived in a small Spanish port called Palos (PAH•los). I liked to stroll down to the harbor and listen to the sailors' reports about their voyages. I never grew weary of their tales, for I wanted to be a sailor, too! I got my chance when Papá took a job on the *Santa María* (SAHN•tah mah•REE•ah).

Undoubtedly you have heard of that ship. It, along with the *Pinta* (PEEN•tah) and the *Niña* (NEEN•yah), sailed under the command of our Captain General, Christopher Columbus. Although he didn't plan it that way, the trip led to the settlement of the New World!

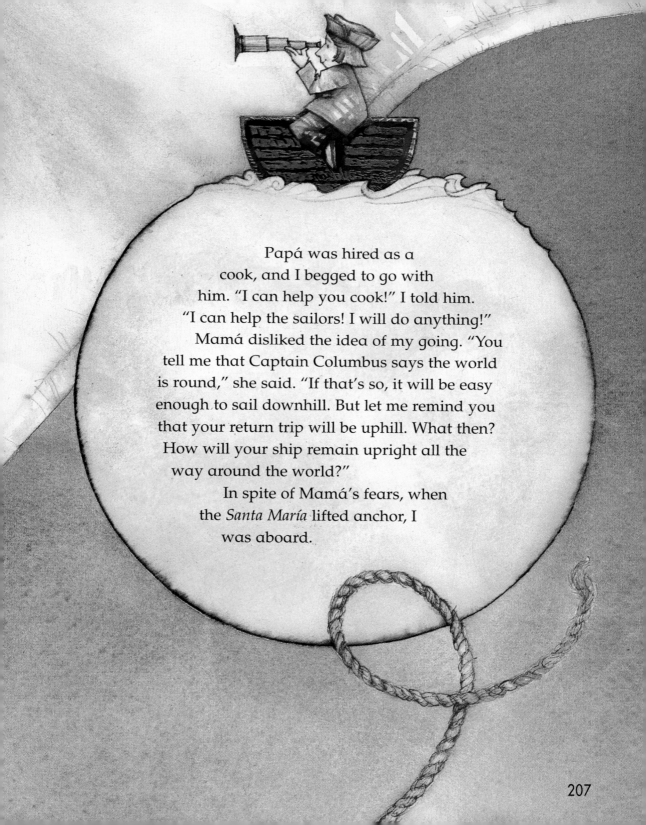

Papá was hired as a
cook, and I begged to go with
him. "I can help you cook!" I told him.
"I can help the sailors! I will do anything!"
Mamá disliked the idea of my going. "You
tell me that Captain Columbus says the world
is round," she said. "If that's so, it will be easy
enough to sail downhill. But let me remind you
that your return trip will be uphill. What then?
How will your ship remain upright all the
way around the world?"
In spite of Mamá's fears, when
the *Santa María* lifted anchor, I
was aboard.

As we left the harbor, I waved to my unhappy
mamá until she faded into the horizon. Then I
turned my back on the land and gazed upon the
calm waters of the vast blue sea.

My job was to help Papá cook. In my spare time
I helped the crew. I scrubbed the deck, I tied and
untied ropes, and I carried buckets of water. Though
the sailors liked me, they often teased me for being
small. This didn't discourage me in the least.

One day a terrible storm came up. Waves nearly flooded the deck, and the ship tipped left and right, struggling to stay upright. Water seeping between the beams made us fear that the ship would sink. Danger from the storm lurked everywhere.

Suddenly, a strong gust of wind caught the sails and almost tipped us over. The storm had come upon us so quickly that there had been no time to lower the sails.

Unless the sails were lowered quickly, the ship would capsize, and we would all drown. It was unsafe, however, to clamber about in the rigging in the midst of a storm. No one dared go up there for fear of falling into the sea—no one but me. Up the mast I shinnied, as bold as a monkey.

When the sails were lowered, the ship was no longer unsteady and water no longer seeped in. Weary sailors furled the sails and stowed them safely. We all huddled below the deck. "Thank goodness for one bold sailor in the crew!" they said—meaning me!

Finally, the sun came out and the winds became calm. It was then that the captain sent for me.

The captain of our ship was Columbus himself. He put one arm around me and swept the other arm to the west. "Look!" he said to me. "Land! Yonder lies our safe harbor. When we drop anchor and go ashore, I will repay you properly. Until then, though, please accept the deepest thanks of your captain and shipmates. You have saved our lives."

My shipmates cheered, and I was a sailor at last.

Think About It

1. How does Manolo Sánchez become a real sailor?

2. After Manolo saves the ship, do you think the sailors feel bad that they had teased him? Why or why not?

3. On the day Manolo saves the ship, his father writes in his diary. He describes what happened and how he felt. Write the diary entry.

Summarize/Paraphrase

Summarizing and paraphrasing are two skills that can help you understand and remember what you read.

When you **summarize** a story or a selection, you retell just its main events. You give only the most important information. A summary of a story is much shorter than the original.

When you **paraphrase** a story or a selection, you retell all of it in your own words. A paraphrase of a story is about the same length as the original.

Read the sentences about "A Safe Harbor." Are they a summary or a paraphrase of the story? How can you tell?

When he was a boy, Manolo Sánchez wanted to be a sailor. He went along on one of Columbus's ships to help his father, the ship's cook. The sailors liked Manolo, but they teased him. When a big storm came up, Manolo climbed the mast to lower the sails. He saved the ship and its crew.

With a partner, choose one of the longer paragraphs in "A Safe Harbor." Together, write a summary of the paragraph. Your summary should have one or two sentences. Then work together to paraphrase the paragraph. Your paraphrase should be about the same length as the paragraph in the story, but it should be in your own words.

Who Was Poor Richard?

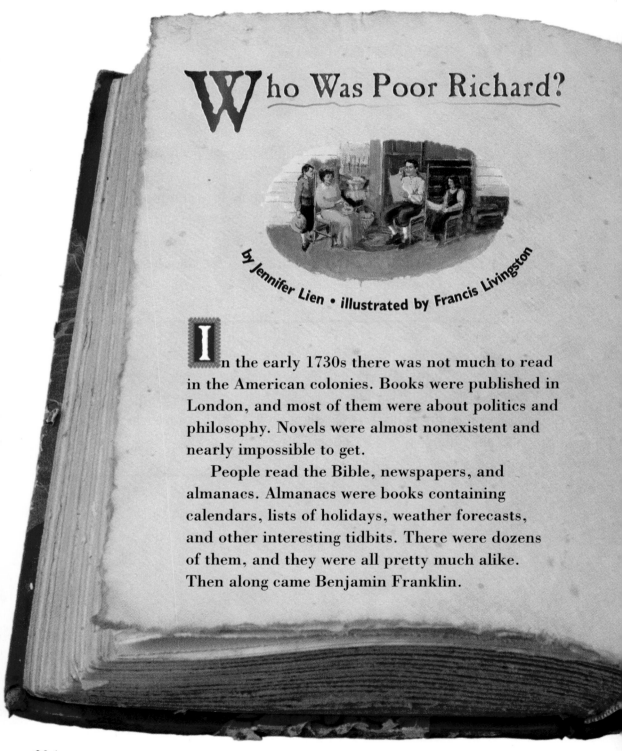

by Jennifer Lien • illustrated by Francis Livingston

In the early 1730s there was not much to read in the American colonies. Books were published in London, and most of them were about politics and philosophy. Novels were almost nonexistent and nearly impossible to get.

People read the Bible, newspapers, and almanacs. Almanacs were books containing calendars, lists of holidays, weather forecasts, and other interesting tidbits. There were dozens of them, and they were all pretty much alike. Then along came Benjamin Franklin.

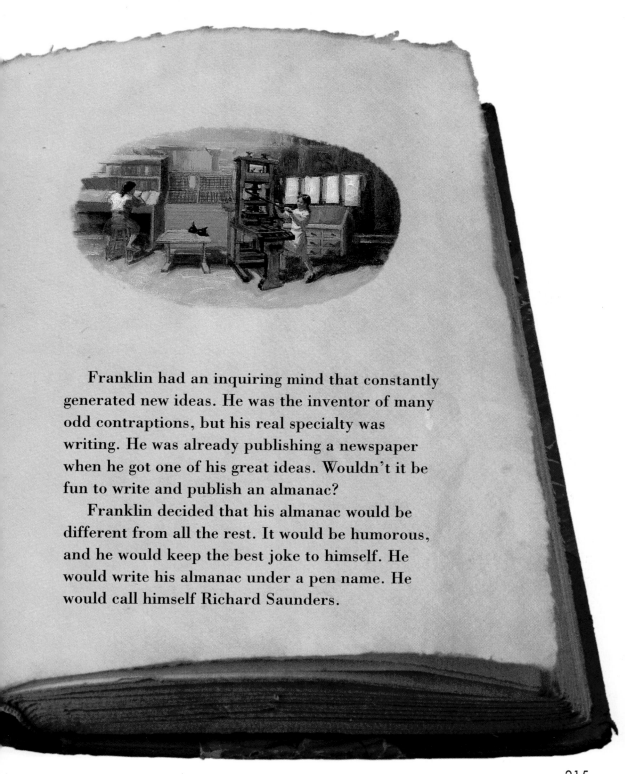

Franklin had an inquiring mind that constantly generated new ideas. He was the inventor of many odd contraptions, but his real specialty was writing. He was already publishing a newspaper when he got one of his great ideas. Wouldn't it be fun to write and publish an almanac?

Franklin decided that his almanac would be different from all the rest. It would be humorous, and he would keep the best joke to himself. He would write his almanac under a pen name. He would call himself Richard Saunders.

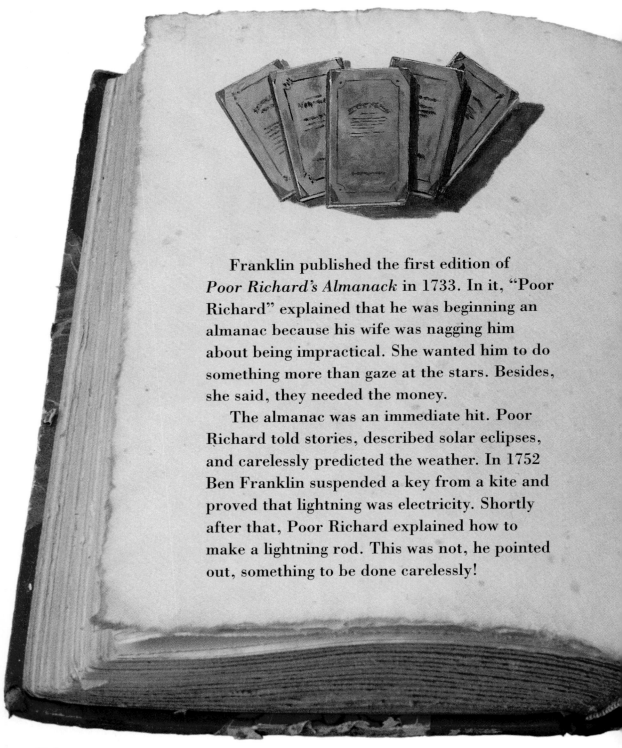

Franklin published the first edition of *Poor Richard's Almanack* in 1733. In it, "Poor Richard" explained that he was beginning an almanac because his wife was nagging him about being impractical. She wanted him to do something more than gaze at the stars. Besides, she said, they needed the money.

The almanac was an immediate hit. Poor Richard told stories, described solar eclipses, and carelessly predicted the weather. In 1752 Ben Franklin suspended a key from a kite and proved that lightning was electricity. Shortly after that, Poor Richard explained how to make a lightning rod. This was not, he pointed out, something to be done carelessly!

The almanac became known for something else. Poor Richard's new specialty was writing proverbs. His way of giving advice through short, humorous sayings brought nods and smiles from those who read them.

Here are a few that he published:

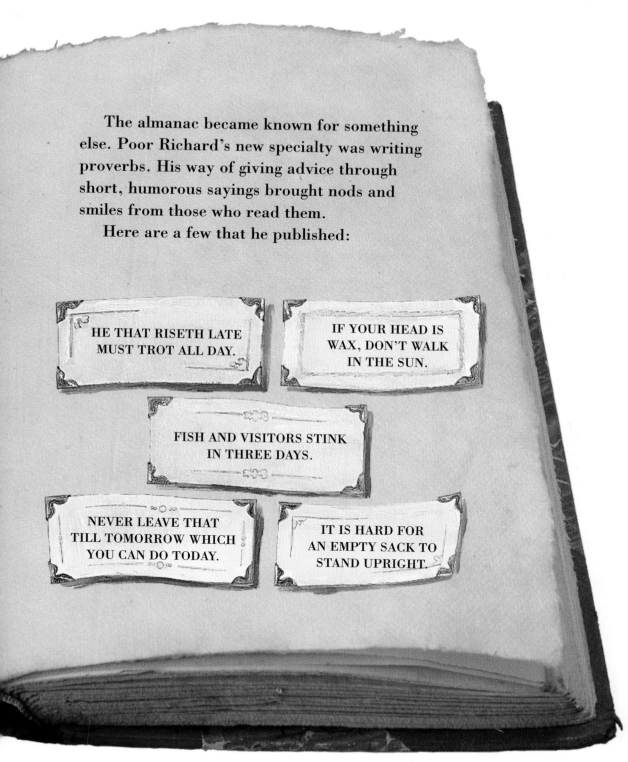

HE THAT RISETH LATE
MUST TROT ALL DAY.

IF YOUR HEAD IS
WAX, DON'T WALK
IN THE SUN.

FISH AND VISITORS STINK
IN THREE DAYS.

NEVER LEAVE THAT
TILL TOMORROW WHICH
YOU CAN DO TODAY.

IT IS HARD FOR
AN EMPTY SACK TO
STAND UPRIGHT.

Ben Franklin wrote *Poor Richard's Almanack* for 25 years. He sold more than 10,000 copies of it every year.

In 1757, Benjamin Franklin had to leave for England on business. He knew he would not be able to write the almanac while he was away.

Before he left, Franklin collected 100 of his favorite sayings. He published them as a preface in the front of the last edition of *Poor Richard's Almanack*. This preface immediately became very popular by itself.

During his long life, Benjamin Franklin won
many honors. In addition to being a writer and
an inventor, he was a very skilled diplomat. He
worked on many important matters. He got the
British to repeal some of their taxes on the colonies.
He helped draft the Declaration of Independence,
too. (Some people were afraid to let him write it for
fear he might conceal a joke in it!) After the
colonies won their independence from England,
Benjamin Franklin helped write the peace treaty.

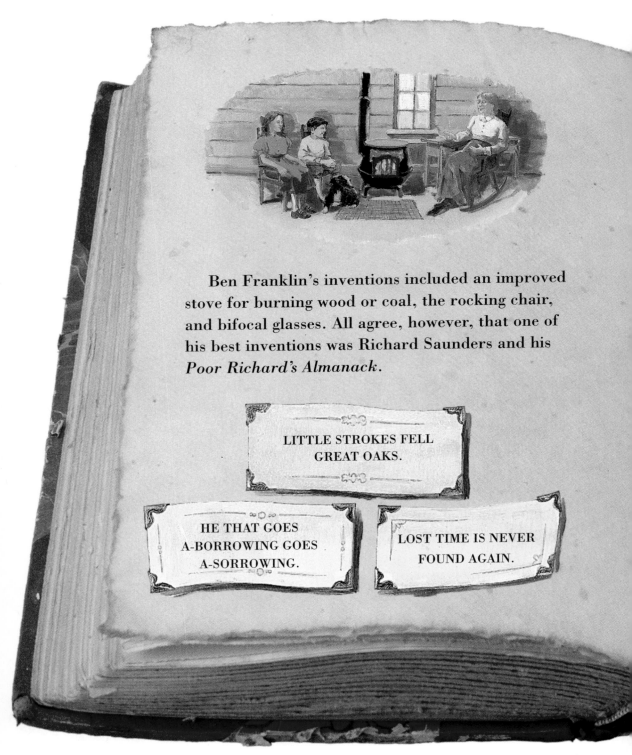

Ben Franklin's inventions included an improved stove for burning wood or coal, the rocking chair, and bifocal glasses. All agree, however, that one of his best inventions was Richard Saunders and his *Poor Richard's Almanack*.

LITTLE STROKES FELL
GREAT OAKS.

HE THAT GOES
A-BORROWING GOES
A-SORROWING.

LOST TIME IS NEVER
FOUND AGAIN.

Think About It

1. Who was Poor Richard? What did he do?

2. Why do you think Franklin chose to give advice in short, humorous sayings?

3. A newspaper might have printed an article about the last edition of *Poor Richard's Almanack*. Write a story that a newspaper could have printed.

Frontier

by Kana Riley

The sun rises over a sea of grass that stretches in endless waves across the plains. The light wakes the children and they crawl out from under their comfortable quilts and dress quickly. It is time to do the chores.

At first the children yawn and blink sleepily. Outside their sod home, however, their energy is restored by the fresh air, and they shiver in the early morning chill. Fall comes early in this climate, and soon the grass will be covered with snow.

Children

The girl grabs a milk pail and a three-legged stool. Her designated chore is to milk the cow that waits in the small barn. Like the house, the barn is made of chunks of sod cut from the grassland.

The girl's younger brother tosses handfuls of corn to the chickens and then feeds the mule. The hungry animals crowd around him trustingly.

Both children work quickly because today is a school day, and they don't want to be late. They will be sorry when snow blocks the road to the schoolhouse. Then they will have to stay home.

Children living on farms today are still expected to be capable helpers.

The climate of the plains is often harsh. In winter the snow-covered plains can seem empty and desolate.

This will be the family's second winter on the plains. Two summers ago they crossed the country in a wagon train as part of the great exodus from the East. Hundreds of families migrated to the West to find good farming land.

When they got to their land, it seemed to the children a useless and desolate place—not a single tree grew anywhere. Their father had dug a hole into the side of a hill, the way a burrowing animal does. He had walled up the open

side, and that's where they had spent the first winter.

Their home back East had been in a town. The children didn't know if they'd like homesteading in a community where friends and farms were miles apart.

Finally spring came, and the family set to work to construct a proper house. In other parts of the frontier, people lived in adobe houses or log cabins. On the plains, there was no clay for making adobe bricks, and there were no trees to provide logs for a cabin. The new home would be a "soddy," built of bricks cut from the sod.

As soon as the sod home was finished, the family turned to planting crops. The parents plowed the land, and the children planted seeds and hauled water.

In the fall the whole family harvested the crops. They put some foods aside for winter and sold the rest in town. They earned enough money to pay the first installment on the loan they had taken for the land.

Some farmers still use horse-drawn plows to cut through sod.

"Breakfast!" the children's mother calls. This morning it's homemade bread and jam. The girl smiles, remembering the pailful of berries she collected to make the jam.

Their mother puts a hard-boiled egg in each of their lunch pails. "Fresh from your chickens," the boy's father says to him with a smile.

The girl helps her brother onto the mule and climbs up behind him. Riding to school is certainly better than walking!

At the schoolhouse, children are playing Snap-the-Whip before school begins. They have formed a long line, holding hands. The leader pulls the line in fast turns, trying to make those on the end lose their grip.

The girl and boy join in the friendly game. Running and shouting with their new friends, they forget how desolate this homesteading community once seemed to them. Now it is home.

One teacher taught children of all ages who attended this one-room sod schoolhouse.

Think About It

1. How is the family's frontier house different from their old house?

2. How do you think the girl and boy feel about doing their chores?

3. The girl sends a letter to a friend back in the town her family left. She tells her friend about her new life on the plains. Write the letter the girl sends.

Main Idea and Supporting Details

Thinking about the main idea and supporting details can help you understand what you read.

You can identify the **main idea** of a paragraph or story by answering the question *What is this mostly about?*

The **supporting details** give more information about the main idea.

This chart shows the main idea and supporting details of the second page of "Frontier Children."

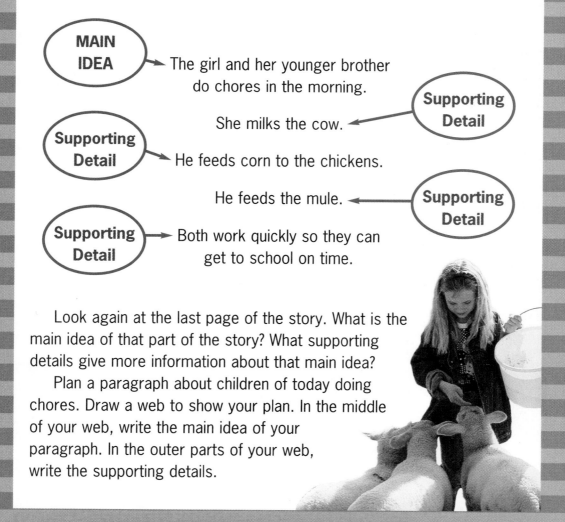

MAIN IDEA → The girl and her younger brother do chores in the morning.

She milks the cow. ← **Supporting Detail**

Supporting Detail → He feeds corn to the chickens.

He feeds the mule. ← **Supporting Detail**

Supporting Detail → Both work quickly so they can get to school on time.

Look again at the last page of the story. What is the main idea of that part of the story? What supporting details give more information about that main idea?

Plan a paragraph about children of today doing chores. Draw a web to show your plan. In the middle of your web, write the main idea of your paragraph. In the outer parts of your web, write the supporting details.

BLACK COWBOYS

by Sydnie Meltzer Kleinhenz   **illustrated by Elizabeth Rosen**

Dad finished his beans as Renata brushed crumbs of cornbread from her Western duds. She wanted to look good riding past the crowds into Houston.

Renata and Dad had joined other African Americans on an eighty-seven-mile trail ride. They had come all the way from Prairie View, Texas, for the Houston Livestock Show and Rodeo. In regular life Dad was a computer programmer, and Renata, of course, was a student. For a couple of weeks each February, however, he and Renata led the trail life of cowboys of the 1800s. Soon their group would join up with groups riding in from fourteen other cities.

Renata and Dad mounted their horses. "Will you tell me some cowboy stories while we ride?" Renata asked. Dad smiled. "I like true stories the best," he said. "I'll tell you some about black cowboys. After the Civil War ended, many discharged soldiers and freed slaves became cowboys. Black men could earn money and respect by being good wranglers.

"One former slave, Bose Ikard, was hired by Charles Goodnight, who helped blaze a cattle trail to Colorado. Goodnight recognized Ikard's roping and riding talents. In addition, he noticed that this cowboy was uncommonly reliable.

"On one occasion, Ikard saved his boss from an Indian attack and nursed him back to health. Several times he stopped stampedes. As Goodnight's business flourished, he trusted Ikard to carry huge sums of money for him. The black cowboy and the wealthy white cattle rancher became close friends, which did not happen often in those times. When Ikard died, Goodnight put up a stone marker with a fond and respectful inscription about his friend."

Renata's horse, Golden, neighed as they trotted in the procession. "Golden wants another story," she said with a grin.

Dad grinned back and started another. "Nat Love's father died after the Civil War, so Nat earned money for his family by taming wild mustangs. When the family began prospering, he left to join a trail ride. A trail boss tested Love by putting him on a horse known for its mean streak. Love, used to the ways of wild mustangs, stuck to that bucking bronco till it ran out of buck. He was hired on the spot. That was the start of a life of adventure for him.

CATTLE TRAILS

MONTANA
TERRITORY

DAKOTA
TERRITORY

Nat Love won
all the rodeo
events here. → • Deadwood

WYOMING
TERRITORY

NEBRASKA

Cheyenne •

COLORADO

KANSAS

• Abilene

Dodge City •

Nat Love made
trips on this heavily
traveled route.

Bose Ikard
made many
trips on this
trail. →

INDIAN
TERRITORY

NEW
MEXICO
TERRITORY

Abilene •

Bill Pickett
was born
near here.

TEXAS

Austin •

Prairie View •

• Houston

KEY
—— Goodnight-Loving Trail (1866–1875)
—— Chisholm Trail (1867–1884)

Brownsville •

"Hunting for strays on the open prairie could be risky. Indians caught Love one time and wanted him to live with them. He did for a while, but in time he decided to return to the life he knew best. Another time his horse bucked him off and left him alone on the prairie. That night it turned freezing cold, and Love was out there with no cold-weather duds. He killed a stray calf for food and took shelter inside its carcass. The next morning his pals found him nearly frozen.

"Love gained a reputation as a top wrangler at a rodeo in Deadwood, South Dakota. He won every single event!

"Years later, he wrote a book called *The Life and Adventures of Nat Love*. People enjoyed his stories and didn't mind that he threw in a little exaggeration here and there."

Seeing Renata's eager expression, Dad went on with his own stories. "The era of cattle drives lasted only about 30 years. The longhorns flourished then because they had the stamina for the long trails. Once cattle needed to be herded only to the nearest railroad station, the longhorns' stamina was no longer needed. Besides, their long horns made them hard to fit into boxcars! Ranchers switched to domesticated cattle, which produced more beef. With no more cattle drives to ride, cowboys turned their attention to rodeo contests.

"And then there was Bill Pickett. He was small, wiry, and known around the rodeos for wrestling steers. Pickett was the first black cowboy to be inducted into the National Cowboy Hall of Fame."

"Is our family descended from a cowboy?" Renata asked.

Dad held out his hat. "No, but we're wearing hats named after Hall-of-Fame bull rider Myrtis Dightman. Dightman taught Charles Sampson, the first black cowboy to win a world championship."

Renata sat taller in her saddle as she waved to the crowds. She might not be a descendant, but she could show her pride in the heritage of the black cowboys!

Think About It

1. Why did many discharged soldiers and freed slaves become cowboys after the Civil War ended?

2. Why do you suppose Renata's dad likes to tell her true stories?

3. Before Renata and her dad leave Houston, she writes a postcard to her best friend back in Prairie View. She describes some of her experiences on the trail. Write a message for Renata's postcard.

THE MYSTERY GUEST

by KAYE GAGER

Time: *1850*
Place: *The Motts's Pennsylvania home*